FIVE YEARS OR SO

RETURN TO LIGHTHOUSE POINT

KAY CORRELL

ZURA LU PUBLISHING LLC

Published by Zura Lu Publishing LLC

071720

This book is dedicated to all those dogs and puppies who bring us such joy in our lives.

KAY'S BOOKS

Find more information on all my books at
kaycorrell.com

COMFORT CROSSING ~ THE SERIES
The Shop on Main - Book One
The Memory Box - Book Two
The Christmas Cottage - A Holiday Novella
(Book 2.5)
The Letter - Book Three
The Christmas Scarf - A Holiday Novella
(Book 3.5)
The Magnolia Cafe - Book Four
The Unexpected Wedding - Book Five

The Wedding in the Grove - (a crossover short

story between series - with Josephine and Paul from The Letter.)

LIGHTHOUSE POINT ~ THE SERIES
Wish Upon a Shell - Book One
Wedding on the Beach - Book Two
Love at the Lighthouse - Book Three
Cottage near the Point - Book Four
Return to the Island - Book Five
Bungalow by the Bay - Book Six

CHARMING INN ~ Return to Lighthouse Point
One Simple Wish - Book One
Two of a Kind - Book Two
Three Little Things - Book Three
Four Short Weeks - Book Four
Five Years or So - Book Five
Six Hours Away - Book Six
Charming Christmas - Book Seven

SWEET RIVER ~ THE SERIES
A Dream to Believe in - Book One
A Memory to Cherish - Book Two
A Song to Remember - Book Three
A Time to Forgive - Book Four
A Summer of Secrets - Book Five

A Moment in the Moonlight - Book Six

INDIGO BAY ~ A multi-author sweet romance series

Sweet Days by the Bay - Kay's Complete Collection of stories in the Indigo Bay series

Or buy them separately:

Sweet Sunrise - Book Three
Sweet Holiday Memories - A short holiday story
Sweet Starlight - Book Nine

Sign up for my newsletter at my website *kaycorrell.com* to make sure you don't miss any new releases or sales.

CHAPTER 1

R obin Baker climbed the stairs to The Nest, the area of Charming Inn that Lillian Charm shared with her niece, Sara. Or used to share.

Sara had just moved into Noah's house after marrying him. Now Lillian lived here alone. Or would for a few more weeks, since she was marrying Gary at the end of the month and he would be moving in.

Sara opened the door and tugged on her hand. "Come in. Charlotte and Ruby are here. You should see the dress Ruby is making for Aunt Lillian. It's gorgeous."

Robin followed Sara to the main room where Lillian stood on a chair while Ruby pinned up the hem of Lil's wedding dress.

"Oh, Lillian, it's gorgeous." Robin gasped. "You look beautiful."

Lillian blushed. "Well, it's Ruby's handiwork that made the dress so special."

"She did a great job. The dress is perfect for you." Charlotte stood to one side, her head tilted, as she eyed the dress. "That little bit of lace. Is that…"

Lillian nodded. "I didn't really want lace, but Ruby saved some of the lace from my sister's wedding dress. You know, the one she remade for Sara, and she used it on mine. I love it. Just a touch of lace."

"That's so nice." Robin eyed the simple white dress with the tiny lace inset in the bodice.

"I'll feel like my sister is here in a way."

"Just like I felt Mom was at my wedding," Sara agreed.

"I love the style you came up with, Ruby. Simple, understated, but classic. And it's very you, Lil." Charlotte slowly circled Lillian, eyeing the dress from every angle.

"And Charlotte is the best judge of clothes," Sara added.

Ruby stood and stretched. "Okay, you can get down from the chair now. All pinned up."

Sara and Robin rushed over to give Lillian a hand.

"I've got it." Lillian admonished them.

"You don't want to fall again. Not just weeks from your wedding." Sara still held out a hand.

"Okay, okay." Lillian took their hands and climbed off the chair. "Let me go slip out of this, and we can go sit outside with some sweet tea."

Robin watched Lillian leave to change, her heart full of love for the older woman and the fact that she had found love. It was something to believe in that people could find true love at any stage in their lives. Lillian and Gary were proof of that. Ah, maybe she was just in a sappy mood today. She was just blissfully happy for Sara, for Lillian... and maybe there was hope that she'd find this illusive love some day.

Lillian changed clothes, and they all went out to the deck with their tea. A warm breeze blew in from the sea and a large umbrella blocked the sun on one end of the deck. They settled onto the cushioned chairs in the shade.

"Do you have most of the decisions made for the wedding?" Charlotte asked.

"I do. I'm getting married here at the inn, of

course. Jay is doing a simple buffet for the reception. I ordered white hydrangeas for flowers... with some teal flowers added in."

Robin grinned. "Of course, you've got to have your teal."

"She's wearing teal flats with her wedding dress." Sara's mouth curved in a smile. "And we're having teal bows tied on the chairs out on the beach."

Lillian shrugged. "What can I say, I love teal."

"And such a well kept secret." Robin looked at the teal cushions they sat on and the off-white umbrella with teal trim spread above them. Not to mention inside The Nest—teal picture frames crowded Lillian's shelves and the vases scattered around were all various shades of teal.

"Charlotte helped me get the invitations out. Her handwriting is so beautiful. Though we're just having family and a few close friends."

"Yes, how did you get away with a smaller wedding than mine? Our wedding list just kept growing and growing." Sara shook her head.

"I just want it small. And Gary is only having his son, Mason. He said he didn't really have more friends to invite and didn't want to start inviting business associates."

"Is he going to commute back and forth from Seattle for work like Julie's husband Reed does?" Charlotte took a sip of her tea.

"Hey, maybe they could 'jetpool'. Is that a thing?" Sara laughed.

"So far Mason hasn't convinced Gary to go back as CEO. So I'm really not sure how that's all going to work out. Gary says he loves living here on the island."

Robin understood that feeling. She couldn't imagine living anywhere else. She adored Belle Island and had lived here her whole life. She glanced out at the water and caught a group of seagulls swooping by in the wind. The waves danced to shore in the easterly wind today. A beautiful day on the island.

She set her glass down. "I should go. I'm working the dining room tonight."

"She took my shift because Gary is taking me to dinner." Lillian tossed out a small laugh, then shrugged. "Or maybe it's because I've been so scattered with all the wedding planning. Yesterday I gave the same room to two different couples. I can't remember ever doing that before. And when a couple asked for a table by the window in the dining room last night, I told them sure… then seated them in the middle of the room."

"You're entitled to have your mind on the wedding instead of the inn. You just let me take care of things at the inn while you concentrate on the wedding."

"You're the best hire I've ever made, Robin. Don't know what I'd do without you."

"Don't let Jay hear you say that. He's convinced he's the best hire you've ever made." Robin grinned and headed to the main part of the inn.

Jay Turner knew he should give the new assistant cook more responsibility. Okay, not really *new*. Dana, the cook they'd hired almost a year ago, was competent enough. He just didn't like to turn over many—if any—of the responsibilities in the kitchen.

She'd offered to help with ordering and making menu plans for events. He'd turned her down, of course. That was his job.

He grudgingly admitted she could now make his cinnamon roll recipe and no one would know the difference. He'd been training her on pie crusts, and she did make a good one —not as good as his, but good. And he wouldn't admit it to anyone, but Dana's sourdough bread was better than any he'd ever made. It annoyed him slightly, but at least they had great sourdough bread and rolls to serve.

They had other help in the kitchen, too. A couple people who cleared tables and ran the dishes and served the food. Extra help on the weekends or during events who did whatever job he barked at them to do. He'd been told he wasn't the easiest boss ever. Robin never failed to remind him of that fact. But he didn't ask any more of them than he asked of himself.

He pushed away from the computer in the corner of the kitchen where he'd double-checked the orders for Lillian's wedding. He would let nothing go wrong for her wedding. He owed her so much. She'd given him this job and trusted him when no one else would. And he could spend forever paying her back for that great kindness and still not feel like he'd done enough. She'd allowed him to turn his whole life around, and he loved the life he'd finally made for himself here on the island.

Robin breezed into the kitchen, snagged a sugar cookie, and came over to him. Her shoulder-length blonde hair was pulled back today in some kind of twist thing. "Everything going okay in here?"

"Of course. Just checking on the orders for Lillian's wedding."

"I just saw the wedding dress Ruby is making her. It's gorgeous."

He didn't doubt that Lillian would look beautiful. She was that type of woman who looked healthy and fit, and her eyes sparkled with warmth. The type of person everyone loved. Okay, he might be a bit biased because he adored the woman. He was so glad that she and Gary had found each other. He'd thought she'd be a confirmed single person for life. That had all changed when Gary came to the island.

Robin tapped his shoulder. "Where did you go?"

"What? Oh, just thinking about wedding things. I want everything perfect for Lillian."

"I'm sure they will be. Your food never disappoints. You're a fabulous chef."

"I'm okay." He shrugged.

"You're great. And you're still horrible at taking compliments." She slapped his arm playfully and walked away, snagging another cookie as she left the kitchen.

He grinned at her retreating back. There was really no reason to argue with Robin. She always won.

Robin stacked dirty dishes onto a tray after the last customers left the dining room. They'd had a good crowd as usual. Jay's cooking was well-loved by the locals as well as the tourists who came to the island. She bumped open the door to the kitchen, balancing the tray on one hip.

Jay looked up from where he was cleaning up the kitchen. "Last one?"

"Yep."

"I'll just rinse those off and run them through the dishwasher in the morning." He nodded toward the washing station.

"I can do that while you finish what you're doing."

"You don't have to."

"I offered." She headed over to the dishwashing station with the dirty dishes and rinsed them all while Jay finished his chores. She finished first and perched on a stool beside the counter, watching him work.

"The rosemary chicken special was a big hit."

"My grandmother's recipe." Jay paused in wiping down the counter. "Though I hate it when I run out of the special before the night is over. I'll have to plan better when I do it again." He scowled.

She knew how he prided himself on estimating the right amount of food for his specials each day. She laughed. "So this is what, the first time in weeks—maybe months—you've been off on your estimate?"

He looked at her with an incredulous expression. "I still hate it."

She got up off the stool. "You're too hard on yourself."

"No, I just expect to get it right."

"Too hard on yourself," she repeated. "I should head home."

"I'm finished here, I'll walk home with you."

She quickly hid her pleased smile. She enjoyed their walks home after they finished their work at the inn. It didn't mean anything, though. They just both lived in the same direction, but she did enjoy his company.

Jay hung up the towel he was using and glanced around the kitchen. She knew he was running through his close-up checklist in his mind. He led her to the back door, locked it behind him, and they headed out.

The night sky was filled with stars and streaked with a few thin clouds drifting across the heavens. A light breeze blew in from the sea. She loved nights like this on the island when the breeze blew away the day's humidity.

They fell into step, walking in and out of the light of the street lamps.

"So, you working early tomorrow?" Jay asked.

"I'm headed over to the mainland tomorrow. I've got errands to run. I'll be back at the inn by early afternoon, I hope."

"That's surprising. You usually work twelve-hour days. At least."

"You're one to talk. You're at the inn before me and leave after the dinner crowd."

"What can I say? I love my job."

"You ever going to let Dana take over more so you can cut back a bit?" She eyed him.

"Probably." He shrugged and his t-shirt stretched across his broad chest. Not that she noticed.

"No, you're not."

He pointed to his t-shirt. She glanced at the shirt, just noticing the saying on it. *The correct answer is: Yes, Chef.*

She grinned at him. "Okay, yes, chef. But I don't mean it."

CHAPTER 2

The next day Robin headed to the mainland with one main objective—find a dress to wear to Lillian's wedding. Nothing in her closet had seemed right. Or she'd worn it a dozen times before, which rarely bothered her, but she wanted something special this time. While they did have a few clothing stores on the island, she'd scoured their racks several times over already, with no luck.

Once on the mainland, she tried on a dozen dresses and couldn't make a decision. This one was too fancy, that one wasn't fancy enough. And one dress she couldn't decide if it was fashionably funky or maybe weird funky and didn't trust her own eyes about what looked good on her. She finally realized she should have brought Charlotte with her to help her choose, so she came away empty-handed.

Her stomach growled, and she decided to grab lunch. She sat outside at a new trendy restaurant just over the bridge from Belle Island. She wanted to check out the place to see how it compared with their dining room at Charming Inn. Not that the dining room would ever try to be a trendy place, but it didn't hurt to check out the competition.

She looked over the menu and grudgingly admired their choices. They'd put some interesting combinations together. Between the menu and the fabulous view of the harbor, she could see how they'd become so popular so quickly.

She looked up from her menu when she felt someone standing beside her table.

"Hey, Robin."

"Mason, what are you doing here?"

"I'm just driving in from the airport. Coming early for Dad and Lillian's wedding. Got hungry and saw the signs for this place and stopped in. I saw you when I walked in and thought I'd come over and say hi."

"I haven't even ordered yet. Do you want to join me?"

Mason's eyes lit up. "Love to."

She motioned to the seat across from her. Mason sat down and waved to the waitress who brought him a menu.

"They've got some good-looking things on the menu. It's going to be hard to decide." Mason looked up from the menu and smiled at her.

"I was just thinking the same thing."

Once again she thought about how much he looked like his father. Same warm brown eyes. Same strong cheekbones. Same brown hair— though no hints of gray in Mason's hair like his father had. He was dressed in khaki slacks and a long-sleeved button-down shirt with the sleeves rolled up. A bit overdressed for the weather here, but the restaurant had an awning covering the tables, and a nice breeze blew off the harbor.

She'd gone out with Mason a few times when he'd first come to the island. Well, not really gone out-gone out. Just hung out a few times. She'd shown him around the island and they'd had dinner a few times. She enjoyed his company, and he really didn't know anyone else on the island, so it was the friendly thing to do.

"So how are the wedding plans coming

along?" Mason asked. "Dad seemed a bit overwhelmed but happy when I talked to him. So I decided to come in early and surprise him. I'll stay until after the wedding. Maybe I can help out some?"

"Everything seems to be going fine. Lillian has everything planned. It's just putting the final touches on things and then making sure everything goes smoothly on the wedding day. Charlotte and I are doing that. Sara is her maid of honor—well, matron of honor I guess since she just married Noah."

"Dad said he's debating between a suit and just a coat and tie. I brought both." He grinned.

"Lillian told him a jacket and slacks would be fine, or even just a dress shirt and slacks, but he seems to want to wear a suit. Either way, he's going to be very warm." She shook her head.

"I hope he opts for shirt and slacks." Mason's warm brown eyes sparkled. "I'm not big on being overly warm at weddings."

They ordered their meals and sat sipping on sweet tea while they waited for their food.

"So, what are you doing on the mainland? I thought islanders rarely left the island. Some kind of code or something." His mouth curved with a teasing smile.

"Well, it has to be an emergency," she said gravely.

"Oh, and the emergency?"

"I needed a dress for the wedding." She grinned. "But, unfortunately, I'm going to have to repeat the emergency trip again because I didn't find anything. I just couldn't make up my mind."

"So, a traitor to the island twice." He winked.

"It appears so." She'd forgotten how effortless it was to talk to Mason and his easy, teasing conversations.

They ate their lunch while chatting away about all things wedding.

"I finally feel caught up on wedding news." Mason's quick smile accentuated his one dimple. "I'm hoping Dad has time to work with me some on GJ Industries business."

"Has he decided whether he's coming back as the CEO?"

"I can't get him to give me a decision. I figure with the wedding and everything I'll give him time. But I could really use him back at work." Mason frowned. "Unfortunately, he not only fell in love with Lillian, he fell in love with your island."

17

"There's lots to love. And I don't think it's unfortunate he fell in love with Lillian or the island."

"I didn't mean…" Mason sighed. "I'm happy for him. I am. But I can't stall the Board of Directors forever. They want a permanent CEO."

"And if he went back to being the CEO, he'd have to be in Seattle all the time, wouldn't he?"

"Not all the time, but quite a bit."

"I'm not sure that will make Gary or Lillian happy."

"Probably not." He glanced at his watch. "I should get to the island."

She stood. "I should head back, too. Got to get to the inn."

He walked her out to her car. "So, would you like to grab dinner while I'm on the island?"

She paused. But what could it hurt? "Sure."

"Tomorrow?" He cocked his head to one side with an impish grin.

"How about Wednesday?"

"I'll take whatever night you'll give me. You're my only friend on the island."

"I should introduce you to more people.

18

Looks like you'll be here more often if your dad is here so much."

"I could get used to being on the island more." He winked again. "Come on, you island traitor, let's get you back home before they send out a search party, hoping you didn't defect to the mainland for good."

JAY SLIPPED onto a stool at the Lucky Duck beside his friends Delbert, Noah, and Ben. He nodded to Willie, the owner, who quickly brought him his favorite beer. After taking a long swig, he turned to his friends. "Long day."

"It's always a long day for you." Noah shook his head. "Sara says you're never going to let that assistant cook take over and give you a break."

"Lillian counts on me." He shrugged. "Besides, I'm letting Dana close up tonight. See?"

Ben glanced at his watch. "No, you waited until the last customer left. So she got to what? Put food away and make sure the dishes were run."

"No, I put the food away."

Noah laughed. "Right. That's giving her a lot of responsibility."

"How about we talk about something else?" Jay scowled at his friends.

"Can we not talk about weddings though? That's all I hear about these days." Noah shook his head. "Between Sara's and mine, and then Lil's and Gary's, it's just all wedding all the time." Noah turned to Ben. "And I guess you and Charlotte will have one soon."

"We haven't set a date. Not yet. Honestly, I'm still getting adjusted to being engaged." Ben turned to Jay. "So you'll be the last bachelor standing. You should ask Robin out."

"How many times do I have to tell you that we're just friends?"

"You can tell me as many times as you want. But I've seen the way you look at her. How she looks at you. You should get over yourself and ask her out." Ben took a sip of his beer. "Like tomorrow. Quit procrastinating. You're driving us all crazy."

Noah laughed. "You really should, you know. It's inevitable."

Jay turned to Delbert. "Don't you want to gang up on me, too?"

Delbert's lips twitched in a smile. "I have to

say, I agree with both of them. I have seen the way you look at her."

"I don't look at her any differently than I look at anyone else."

"False." Noah shook his head.

Jay knew they were wrong. Robin and he were just friends. Good friends, but friends. Co-workers even, since Robin had started working for Lillian, too. And that would just complicate matters if they went out, right? And what if they went out and it all went wrong and then they weren't even friends anymore? How awkward would that be at work?

He shook his head. "So, let's talk about something else."

"Wow, everyone sure is choosy about subjects tonight," Ben teased.

LILLIAN SAT KNITTING LATE that night. Her mind was going a million miles an hour with thoughts of the wedding and things that needed to be done. Usually, knitting would calm her down, but tonight nothing seemed to be working. She set it aside, wondering if she should go to bed and read some more of the journal Gary had found when he was rehabbing Magnolia House for a guesthouse for the inn.

She felt guilty that she'd stalled in her search for the journal's owner, but she didn't think she could concentrate on that either.

The Nest was quiet tonight. Very quiet. She'd gotten used to having Sara with her again, and it was quite the change when she'd moved out with Noah.

She got up and made herself a cup of chamomile tea. That familiar routine soothed her as she heated the water and got out one of her favorite teacups. When the tea was ready, she walked out to the deck and sat under the stars.

She didn't know why she felt so uneasy tonight. Some kind of instinct of hers was on high alert, but she didn't know why. There was a feeling of *something* in the air. A feeling of uncertainty, or even impending danger. Which was silly. She must just be imagining things.

It was probably just so many changes, so quickly. She felt sure she was making the right decision marrying Gary. She was. She just wasn't certain how much of an adjustment it would be having Gary living here with her. She was set in her ways.

Gary had assured her they'd work things out. He'd adapt. She knew she'd adapt, too.

But it was just a lot of change...

She sipped her tea and stared out at the night. She and Gary had talked about him resuming his duties as CEO of GJ Industries, but he hadn't decided what he wanted to do about that.

Maybe it would even be easier to adjust if he were gone to Seattle part of the time. She immediately felt guilty at the thought. And she would miss him. She saw him every day now and loved it. His welcoming smile and his teasing eyes when he joked with her. She loved every single thing about the man.

Yes, it was just a lot of changes all at once. That was all. She got up to go inside to bed. Busy day tomorrow with inn business and wedding things to do. It was just wedding jitters. That must be all it was.

But she couldn't fight off the strange feeling that something was wrong. Or would be wrong soon.

CHAPTER 3

Jay got to the inn early the next morning. It was quiche day at Charming Inn, and he had crusts to make. He looked around the kitchen and saw that Dana had put everything carefully away back in its place when he'd let her close up the kitchen last night. He didn't know whether that pleased him or irritated him.

He pulled out the ingredients and started making the crusts for the quiche. Dana breezed into the kitchen. "Morning, Jay. Want me to make those crusts for you?"

She was in early considering how late she must have been here closing up last night. And he couldn't decide if that pleased or irritated him either. "No, I've got the crusts."

"Okay, what would you like me to start with?"

"Chop up the chicken for the chicken broccoli quiche and chop the tomatoes for the spinach quiche."

"Will do." Dana headed across the kitchen to begin, which suited him fine. He liked his space when he worked.

He methodically made crust after crust all the time thinking about what his friends had said last night. Ask Robin out? He scowled. No, they were just friends, right? Why mess up a good thing? Besides, would she really want to go out with him? They came from different worlds. Hers was normal. His... wasn't. And if she ever found out about his past—well, women like her didn't date people like him.

But maybe he could ask her to do... something. Not a date really. Not like going out to dinner, but *something*.

There was the outside theatre in the park. They played classic movies on Wednesday nights. It might be fun to go to that. He didn't go to current movies, but he did enjoy a classic. Wonder what was playing this week? That seemed like something Robin might like to do, too. Didn't it? And not too date-y.

"You're lost in thought."

He dropped the rolling pin and whirled around to see Robin standing inches from him. "Hey. Don't startle me."

"Sorry." She looked surprised at his short words with her.

"I'm busy, what do you want?" He turned back to the crust-making, avoiding her. Or avoiding asking her to the movie…

"Someone's in a mood today."

"Sorry." He knew his tone didn't sound sorry. *This* is why he shouldn't even think about asking her to do something with him. He got… crazy.

But then, it would be nice to go see the movie with her. As friends, of course. And if he did it, it might get Ben and Noah off his case. That would be a plus. He watched her as she carefully selected a mug and poured in the strong coffee but didn't add any cream or sugar. She liked her coffee black. He knew that much about her. She came back over to lean against the counter.

He gathered his courage. Now or never. "So, Wednesday is usually not very busy here at the inn."

"I know. Which is good because I have

plans. I'm not going to be here Wednesday night."

"You aren't?" He set the rolling pin down and turned to her. "Going out with Sara and Charlotte? You guys haven't had a girls' night out since Sara got married." It figured it would be the same night he wanted to see if she wanted to go to the movie. Just his luck.

"Uh… no." She stared into her coffee cup as if something about it fascinated her. "I… uh…" She looked back up at him. "I'm just meeting Mason for dinner. You know, Gary's son. He's in town and doesn't know anyone and… well… it seemed like the nice thing to do."

"Sure. A nice thing to do." He shrugged. No big deal. Just having dinner with another man. It didn't really matter to him. "Well, Wednesday's a good night to do it."

"Why did you mention Wednesdays being slow nights?" She looked at him.

He searched for an excuse. "Oh, I was thinking I might let Dana have a bit more responsibility on Wednesdays."

"Well, good for you." She gave him a wide smile. "That's great." She started to walk away, then turned to look back at him. "Now we'll see if it really happens."

She walked away, and he watched her every step, keenly aware of the feelings surging through him.

What was he feeling?

He was jealous.

Jealous.

That was ridiculous. She could see whoever she wanted.

But there was no way he was going to leave things up to Dana on Wednesday because now he wanted to stay busy. Super busy. So he wouldn't think about Robin out with that Mason guy. He'd heard Mason was the CEO of some big corporation. He could never compete with that. Robin deserved someone like this Mason guy. Came from money. Probably even wore suits. He glanced down at his t-shirt dusted with flour and his very, *very* worn jeans.

He slammed another chunk of pie dough onto the counter and grabbed the rolling pin, rolling the dough until it was too thin. He sighed and mounded the dough up again to start over. This is what he got for even thinking about her in any way except as a friend. No more. The ridiculous thoughts were over.

They were friends. Period. Nothing else. Nothing else at all.

And he was perfectly fine with that.
Perfectly.

ROBIN COULDN'T SHAKE the feeling that
something was off with Jay this morning. He'd
been so jumpy and then looked... strange...
when she'd told him she was meeting Mason for
dinner.

Not that Jay cared who she ate dinner with,
of course. They were just friends. They'd been
friends for five years or so, ever since he'd come
to the island and started working for Lillian.
They'd become even closer this year now that
they worked together at the inn.

But still, just friends.

She walked over to the reception desk and
checked on things, then poked her head into
Lillian's office. "Everything okay here? Need me
for anything?"

Lillian looked up from her desk. "No...
everything's fine." She frowned. "I think."

She walked into the room and sat on the
chair across from the desk. "What do you mean,
you think?"

"I'm not sure... I just have this... *feeling*. I

don't know what else to call it. And I can't shake it." Lillian's forehead creased. "I know it's kind of silly... but something is off. Almost a premonition or something."

"Wedding jitters?" Robin suggested.

Lillian gave a small smile. "You're probably right. Just nerves."

"You've had a lot of changes in a short time. Sara getting married and moving out. You getting married."

"I'm sure you're right." Lillian's eyes didn't look like she was totally convinced.

"Well, I'll go get to work. Let me know if I can do anything inn-wise or wedding-wise."

"I will."

Robin left the office and went to go check the event calendar. They had dozens of events scheduled for the coming months, and she wanted to make sure she had everything in order for them. She kept a big notebook with a section for each event complete with checklists and phone numbers she might need. And when it got closer to the event time, she always looked at the weather forecast since so many events were held outside and sometimes they put up a large tent to protect people from the elements. Florida weather was always so unpredictable.

She opened the notebook to Lillian's wedding. Two weeks. She punched in the weather on her computer and saw, as of now, the weather would be perfect. Not that a two week out forecast was very accurate, but she hoped Lillian had wonderful weather for her special day.

CHAPTER 4

R obin stood in her bungalow, balancing on one foot, trying to tug on her other flat. She swore it was a size too small.

Charlotte sat on the bed, hugging a throw pillow and eyeing her. "That's the third pair of shoes you've tried on."

"None of them feel comfortable and I'm not sure if I like this outfit."

Charlotte climbed off the bed, tossing the pillow behind her. "I'm not sure why you're so edgy about this date. But here. Let me help."

Charlotte reached into her closet. "Change into this dress. You love it. It's simple and loose and flowy. And wear the red flats."

She looked at Charlotte gratefully and went to slip on the dress Charlotte had picked out for her. The doorbell rang, and she looked at her watch. Six o'clock. Exactly. "Char, can you get that?"

"If you promise to finish getting dressed and quit changing clothes."

"Char, just go answer it." Her friend disappeared out the door.

Robin looked in the mirror. Charlotte was right. The dress was comfortable and not fancy and not too... too what? She shook her head and slipped on her red flats like Charlotte commanded. Why was she even worried about what she was wearing? She would've just gone in her work clothes if not for the fact that she'd managed to spill tea on herself during the lunch shift. Who knew it would be so hard to pick out clothes to wear for a simple dinner in town?

It was just that Mason was so polished and accomplished. A CEO, for Pete's sake. She didn't want to look like some small-town bumpkin. She scowled. Since when did she care that she was born and raised in a small town? She loved Belle Island. She needed to just get over herself.

She grabbed a favorite necklace—a small silver sand dollar on a delicate chain—and slipped it on. There, she was ready.

She walked out into the main room of the bungalow where Charlotte was talking to Mason. He turned and smiled when she entered. "You look nice. Nice dress. Looks great on you."

The hint of a blush heated her cheeks. "Ah… thanks."

Charlotte smothered a laugh.

Mason looked nice himself. More than nice. He had on khaki slacks, a knit collared shirt in navy blue, and expensive looking leather loafers. He looked fresh out of the shower with his hair still slightly damp. As she walked closer, she could smell the faint woodsy scent of his aftershave.

She glanced over at Charlotte and sent her a save-me look. Charlotte just grinned in return. "You two have a fabulous time."

"I'm sure we will. You ready?" Mason offered his arm.

She took his arm and as they started to walk out the door they ran into Ben. He looked at them in surprise, and she had to resist the urge to jerk her hand off Mason's arm.

"Well, hi." Ben looked from Mason to her and back to Mason.

"Ben, this is Mason. Gary's son."

35

Ben reached out a hand. "Right, we met at Sara's wedding."

"Right, I think we did. Though I met like a million people that night. It was nice of Sara to include me." The men shook hands and she could swear they were sizing each other up in that way that men had.

Charlotte walked up behind them. "Well, Sara and you will be kind of family since your dad is marrying her aunt. But don't ask me to figure out what the actual relationship would be." She turned to Robin. "You two go on to your dinner. Ben, come on in." She reached for Ben's hand and tugged him inside.

Robin and Mason headed for the fancy sports car he'd rented. She looked at it and then at him, wanting to ask if he'd like to just walk. But then, he did have on those nice leather shoes…

He opened the car door for her, and she slid inside. He came around and slipped in and they headed to Magic Cafe. Maybe she should have picked an out-of-the-way place to eat. Or even one over on the mainland. People on the island did like to talk, and if they saw her out with Mason, she was sure there would be speculation about what was going on. Which was nothing. Nothing was going on. Nothing at all.

Tally greeted them when they got to Magic Cafe. She already knew Mason, of course. She remembered everyone she'd ever met, it seemed. They took a table near the sand, and Mason ordered a bottle of wine after looking at the list. It was obvious he knew his wines.

They sipped their wine while they waited for their dinner. Mason was easy to talk to. He remembered she hadn't found a dress yet and asked if she'd made any progress on that. No, she hadn't, but Charlotte had promised to go with her later this week to find one.

She really wasn't sure why she'd been in such a tizzy getting ready tonight. He was a nice man. Attentive. Very good-looking. Just a big city CEO and that rattled her a bit, she admitted.

After dinner, they sat watching the sunset as they finished their wine. Robin looked up and saw Camille and Delbert approaching and quickly squared her shoulders and took a deep breath.

"Robin. So nice to see you." Camille put on her trademarked fake smile.

"Camille."

"And Mason, *so good* to see you again." She flashed a perfect smile at Mason, nothing like the one she'd tossed at her. "Do you remember meeting us at Sara and Noah's wedding?"

"Yes, I sure do."

"Delbert, you remember meeting Mason's father, Gary, that CEO who's marrying Lillian. I heard he's quite successful, but there was some kind of scandal... Anyway, I can't believe he'll be happy here on this little island for long." Camille shook her head, and her perfectly curled hair bounced across her shoulders.

How the heck did that woman keep perfect curls in this humidity?

"Gary Jones's son. I believe his company put in some bids on a few hotels we were building." Delbert nodded.

"I think so." Mason nodded. "We didn't get the jobs, though."

Delbert smiled ruefully. "Competition is tough in the hotel building business."

"It is." Mason nodded agreeably.

"It was nice to see you two. Camille, darlin', we should let them finish their meal." Del took Camille by the elbow and led her away to their table across on the far side of the outside seating, thank goodness.

"She's... interesting."

"Quite. She's so full of herself and... well, she says unkind things about Lillian and the inn, and she spread nasty rumors about Sara and... well, lots of reasons that I really don't like her."

"That's a lot of reasons." Mason gave her a lazy smile.

"It is. She told Lillian that it was surprising that she'd get married at her age. Imagine that. She's just so... rude."

"So I take it she won't be at Lillian's and Dad's wedding."

"No, she won't."

"I actually looked up Hamilton Hotels after Dad made some mention about meeting Delbert. He's quite successful and is doing a great job taking over the company from his father." Mason gave a rueful smile. "Probably better than I am at taking over my dad's company."

"Gary says you're doing a great job."

"I still wish he'd come back and take over." He shrugged. "But Dad will do what he wants. What's best. I'm not sure the board of directors won't give the CEO job to an outsider if Dad steps down permanently. That would be... strange. I can't remember a time that it wasn't

Dad's company, run by him. I mean it's named after him for Pete's sake."

"I'm sure your dad will decide soon. Although it may be after the wedding."

"I wonder what Lillian thinks about Dad going back to his job as CEO?"

"I don't know. She hasn't said anything. Knowing Lillian, she'd support whatever decision your dad made and they'd make it work for them."

"You really think highly of her, don't you?"

"I adore her. And she's a sharp businesswoman. And a wonderful friend and was wonderful raising Sara."

"Well, I hope Dad and Lillian are very happy."

"Me, too."

BEN AND CHARLOTTE ate dinner at the inn, then walked back to the bungalow she shared with Robin. Ben had been quiet most of the evening.

"You okay?" she asked as they settled on the weathered bench out on the porch.

"I am. It was just a long day at the marina."

"That's it?"

"Well, I am wondering what's going on with Robin and that Mason guy. You know that Jay has a thing for her, right?"

"Everyone knows that Jay has a thing for her. And she has a thing for Jay. They just never seem to do anything about it."

"I thought we'd talked him into asking her out when we were at the Lucky Duck a few nights ago. I was surprised to see her going on a date with someone else."

"Well, if he isn't going to ask her out, then she should go out with other guys."

"But Jay and Robin... there *is* something going on between them."

"But if neither one of them does anything about their feelings for each other, then nothing will happen between them." Charlotte leaned against Ben, and he circled his arm around her.

"I wonder if Jay knows she has this date?"

"I'm not sure."

Ben turned to look at her. "I'm glad we're past that awkward stage of dating."

"Me, too."

"You know..." He took her hand in his. "We should talk about setting a wedding date."

"We should." She had been thinking about it but wanted to give them both enough time to

41

get adjusted to being engaged. Besides, with the recent rash of four-week weddings, she wanted to take her time with hers. Decide on every little detail.

"I was thinking we shouldn't wait a long time." He eyed her.

"You're not thinking of one of these plan-in-four-weeks weddings, are you? Because that's a big fat no."

He laughed. "No, but how does Christmastime sound?"

She thought for a moment. That was months away. It would give her time to choose everything and deliberate on every decision, which she was sure she would do. Her mother would think it was way too soon, but then, she didn't worry about what her mother thought anymore. She knew some people planned weddings for over a year, but she didn't need that. "Christmas sounds like a lovely time to get married. My parents and sisters are coming for a long visit this weekend. Let's pick the exact date and I'll tell them when they come to town."

He eyed her. "All three are coming? You okay with that?"

"Dad just called today to tell me. He wants to

play in a golf tournament here with his buddies. Dad promised that Mom and Eva will be on their best behavior. They're staying at Charming Inn."

Four days of her family. That could get interesting.

"And we need to think about where we want to live after we get married. Lady Belle would be kind of crowded for the two of us." Ben's thumb brushed back and forth on the back of her hand.

"But you love her."

"Charlotte, I've seen your closet… there's not enough room on the trawler for even your clothes."

She frowned. "I guess I never thought of that."

"And you need somewhere to paint. There's no room for that on the boat, either."

"I guess we should look for a place then…" She worried about him moving off the boat, though. He had such a connection to it, and she knew it made him feel close to his father.

"We don't have to decide where right now. We have time. But we should start looking. Maybe something on the beach? With lots of natural light for your painting?"

"That sounds nice. I'd love to look out over

the beach. Or the bay if that's more convenient to your work."

His mouth curved into a lazy grin. "*Everywhere* on the island is convenient to the marina."

She laughed. "I guess you're right."

"I'm glad we at least came up with when we're getting married."

"I want to get married at the inn. So I'll check with them for exact dates that are available."

"Perfect." He kissed her and stood. "And I should go. Have another long day tomorrow."

She nodded and watched him disappear down the sidewalk back to his beloved Lady Belle. She frowned. That was going to be a hard adjustment for him. Leaving the boat.

A car pulled up and Mason got out and came around to help Robin out of the car. They talked for a minute or two, and Robin came up to the porch and sank into a seat beside her as Mason left.

"Did you have a good time?"

Robin kicked off her shoes and tucked her legs under her. "I did. Mason is fun and easy to talk to."

"Going out with him again?"

"I'm not sure."

"Do you like him?"

"I haven't really thought about it."

Charlotte cocked her head to one side. "Really?"

"Well, not much. I mean he lives across the country and he's this big-shot CEO." She shrugged. "Anyway, I just enjoy his company. That's all."

Charlotte leaned forward. "Well, I have news."

"What's that?"

"Ben and I are getting married at Christmastime."

Robin clapped her hands. "That's wonderful."

"We just need to check the inn's schedule."

"I'll do that first thing when I go in in the morning. A Christmas wedding. That's so romantic." Robin sighed. "Both you and Sara will be married."

"It won't change anything with the three of us," she assured Robin. "But I will be moving out of the bungalow. Are you going to look for a new roommate?"

Robin frowned. "I don't know. I haven't really thought about it. I can swing the rent on my own." She shrugged. "But I admit I do like having you here with me."

"Ben said we might look for a place on the beach."

"Oh, that would be nice."

"I'm worried about him leaving the Lady Belle, though."

"It is his pride and joy."

"And he just recently rehabbed her and moved onto her to live." She looked up at the stars as if they'd give her an answer.

"People have to make changes when they get married. Do things that work for both of them." Robin grinned. "Or so I've been told. I'm not exactly an expert on marriage."

"I'm not either. But I guess we'll both have to make some big adjustments."

Robin stood. "Come on. It's late, let's go inside. You can't make any of these decisions tonight, anyway."

She stood and followed Robin into their bungalow. The first place that had ever felt like home to her, where she belonged. And she'd be leaving it soon.

JAY SAT on a barstool at the Lucky Duck, nursing a beer. He looked up in surprise when Ben slipped onto the stool next to him. "Hey."

"Hey, yourself. Since when do you come here alone? I was walking back to the marina and saw you sitting in here." Ben nodded to Willie to bring him a beer.

"Yeah, well, Lil kicked me out of the kitchen. Said I was in too much of a lousy mood."

"And were you?"

Jay looked at his beer, then back at Ben. He let out a long sigh. "Probably."

"Any reason?"

"Nope, none at all."

"It had nothing to do with Robin?"

Jay eyed his friend. "What do you mean by that?"

"The fact she was out with Mason tonight?"

He scowled. "That has nothing to do with me."

"Right. Nothing." He took the beer from Willie. "So has Jay been here pouting all night?"

Willie grinned. "Pretty much."

"I haven't been pouting. I'm just…" He didn't want to tell them he was mad at himself for not asking Robin out before she started seeing Mason. Mad that Robin would say yes to going out with Mason, even though she had every right to. Mad at himself for being mad.

And he was jealous.

And he was mad about that, too.

Ben pinned him with a look. "You should ask her out, you know."

"So you've said. Probably a million times. But she's seeing this Mason guy now."

"Sometimes you are so—" Ben shrugged. "Ridiculous. Nonsensical. You know you like Robin. Ask. Her. Out."

"I don't want to talk about it anymore." He dropped some bills on the counter to pay for his beer and walked out, leaving Ben to finish his beer on his own. Served him right. Sometimes a man just needed to sit alone without being nagged by a friend who thought he knew best.

Even if the friend was probably right…

CHAPTER 5

J ay was surprised to find Dana already working when he got to the inn the next morning. "Hey, what are you doing here so early?"

"You said we were having cinnamon rolls this morning. Thought I'd get a start on those. And we're running low on sourdough bread, so I'll make that up after the cinnamon rolls." She looked at him. "I hope that's okay?"

"No. I mean, yes. Yes, that's fine."

He crossed over and grabbed things from the fridge that they'd need for breakfast. Possibly using a bit more force than necessary. He knew they probably did need an assistant cook here at the inn, but he loved his early mornings here by himself.

Now Dana was invading his territory.

But Lil kept insisting they needed a backup, and he needed help. He stopped and stared at the eggs and bacon on the counter. Why *was* she so insistent about it? It wasn't like he was going to leave. Like ever.

But was Lil afraid he would leave now that he'd made a name for himself? Or *kind of* a name. At least in the area. And Delbert *had* offered him a job at The Cabot Hotel on Moonbeam Bay. But he'd turned him down. He owed Lillian too much.

He started making batter for pancakes, all the while watching Dana as she hummed —*hummed*—as she made the cinnamon rolls.

It used to be quiet in here in the mornings, too.

Robin breezed into the kitchen, looking for coffee, not five minutes later. Great. Now the women could chat and shatter whatever peace there was left in here. Besides, he wasn't sure he was ready to see Robin. He was still ridiculously mad at her for going out with Mason. Which was crazy. And he hated crazy.

Robin stopped by where Dana was working and did chat with her for a few minutes, of course. Then she headed over to where he was working. "Morning, Jay."

"Hey." He continued working, barely looking up at her. Ignoring the question he wanted to ask her. He wasn't going to ask it, though. Because he didn't really *want* to know how her date with Mason went last night. Just the *thought* of it squeezed his heart.

Unfortunately, she was oblivious to his attempt to shut her out. "Did you hear? Ben and Charlotte decided they were getting married at Christmastime. I need to hop on the computer and look and see what dates we have available. She wants to get married at the inn."

No, Ben hadn't told him that last night at the Lucky Duck, but he hadn't really given him a chance. He'd just up and left, leaving Ben alone with his drink. Some friend he was.

He took a steadying breath and turned to look at Robin instead of being a sullen jerk. Her sparkling emerald eyes almost caught him off guard. Her delicate hands encircled the mug as she took a sip. Her fingernails were painted a rose pink color. He frowned. When was the last time he'd noticed what color her nails were? Ever?

"Jay?"

"What?" He pulled himself away from studying each little detail about her. And why was he scrutinizing them *now*? She was seeing someone now. A foolish time to ask her out. Not that he would ask her out. He set the bowl he was holding down with a clatter. "No, I didn't know they'd decided on a wedding date."

"Well, a time of year, at least. Looks like you'll have another wedding to cook for."

"Looks like." He turned back to the counter and whisked the pancake batter, though it was already stirred. But that was better than his newfound ability to observe every single detail about Robin. Like her hair brushing her shoulders and the slight pink hue of her lipstick. Or the way her skirt flowed around her, hitting just at her knees, and her tanned legs poking out below it with pink flat shoes. Sensible shoes, in his estimation, instead of those ridiculous heels some women liked to wear. Not practical for being on your feet all day.

Why was he thinking about women's shoes?

"Okay... well... I guess I'll let you get back to work."

He didn't miss the slight hurt in her voice.

"Uh-huh."

"I'll let you know what the actual date of their wedding is."

"I'll see it on the calendar."

"Okay, then." Now the hurt came through loud and clear in the soft tones of her voice.

She left the kitchen, and he turned around, staring at where she'd disappeared out the door. He was a jerk. A first-class jerk.

Honestly, she was probably better off without him. Without even being friends with him. Though, double honestly, he was probably just thinking that to protect himself. He didn't like the feeling of his heart being strangled in his chest.

ROBIN LEFT THE KITCHEN, annoyed at Jay. She often stopped by and chatted with him off and on during the day. No need for him to be so rude today. Men. She had no clue why he'd been in such a lousy mood for days now, but she hoped he snapped out of it soon. Poor Dana, working in the kitchen all day with just Jay and his bad attitude.

He'd hopefully get over it soon. He wasn't the most outgoing, friendly guy, but most of that was just a front. She knew he had a kind heart even if he liked to keep that fact hidden.

And he'd really hidden it the last few days…

She headed off to her office, slipped behind the desk, and checked the computer. They had two dates in December that Charlotte could have her wedding. Perfect. She reached for her phone to call Charlotte but paused and laughed when Charlotte poked her head in the doorway.

"I thought I'd come over and see what you found out about available dates."

"First weekend in December, or third weekend."

"Oh, the first weekend. That will be perfect," Charlotte said.

"Looks like you have a wedding date then." Robin keyed it into the computer.

"I have a wedding date." Charlotte looked a bit stunned.

"Yes, you have a wedding date." Robin grinned at her.

"That means I'm really getting married."

"That's what happens when you get engaged and set a wedding date." Robin rolled her eyes.

"I'm going to head to the marina and tell Ben."

"And maybe he'll be in a better mood than his good friend Jay," she mumbled.

"What?" Charlotte eyed her.

"Oh, nothing. It's just that Jay is in some kind of mood today. Has been for a few days. I know he likes his alone time in the kitchen, but I just popped in there to tell him about your wedding and he…" She shrugged. "Never mind, he's just in a bad mood, I guess."

"Or…" Charlotte looked like she wasn't sure of what she was going to say.

"Or what?"

"Or maybe he's a bit jealous that you had that date with Mason?"

"He wouldn't be jealous." She shook her head. "That's crazy. We're friends."

"You know he likes you, don't you?"

"No, he doesn't. Well, he does. We've been friends for five years or so."

"Right. I've seen how he looks at you." Charlotte tilted her head. "He doesn't look at other women that way."

"You're wrong."

"I'm right."

"I know people don't usually win an argument with you… but I *am* right this time." Charlotte turned and left.

"No, you're not," she muttered long after Charlotte had disappeared.

Charlotte wasn't right. Things weren't like that between her and Jay. They weren't. And she wasn't about to lose him as a friend by trying out dating him. What if that didn't work out and she lost him as a friend, too? She'd miss his easy companionship—well, except for the last few days—and they still had to work together here at the inn. How awkward would that be?

Nah, Charlotte was wrong.

CHAPTER 6

J ay banged pots and barked orders at everyone throughout breakfast. Dana finally came over to him with a tentative expression on her face. "Why don't you go take a short break? I'll clean up the breakfast mess and get started on lunch. I've already got the soup going."

He looked across at the large pot on the stove. He hadn't even noticed she'd made the soup. And he hadn't asked her to make it, so why had she? Of course, she could see that vegetable soup was on the menu and they'd talked about it yesterday, but he wasn't totally sure he approved of all this initiative she was taking these days.

He let out a long breath, realizing he was

really the issue, not Dana. "Yeah, maybe I will. I'll be back in a few minutes."

"Take your time. I've got this."

Fine, she had this. He would just go out and take a quick walk on the beach and clear his mind. He headed out the back door and down to the beach. He stood at the edge of the beach in the shade of a trio of palm trees. Going to be a hot one today. The light breeze barely stirred the humidity. It was a much better day for swimming in the ocean than standing here in the heat. For a brief moment he wondered if he had time to go for a swim. Maybe the water would soothe him. He detested being this out of sorts. He glanced back at the inn.

He knew what he really needed to do, and a walk on the beach or a quick swim wouldn't solve it. He needed to go apologize to Robin for being such a jerk. She had every right to date Mason, and he had no right to judge her for it or be so... rude. He *had* been rude. She was his friend. Guilt pinged his every nerve.

Yes, he'd go find her and apologize. He hated feeling like he was on the outs with her. With that settled, he headed back into the inn and found her in the lobby area. "Hey, you."

She turned around. "Hi." She didn't sound

very welcoming, not that he blamed her. Her usual smile was noticeably missing.

"I'm sorry about this morning. I was in a lousy mood."

"You were." She turned away and made a big production about adjusting a picture on the wall that as far as he could tell was perfectly straight to begin with.

Ah, she wasn't going to cut him any slack. Not that he deserved it. He reached out and touched her arm. "No, really, I'm sorry. I was being a jerk."

"Yes, you were." She pulled her arm away.

The sunlight streaming through the window highlighted her blonde hair. And there it was again. Noticing small details about her. He tried again with the apology.

"I'm sorry if I hurt your feelings. You ever going to forgive me?" He gave her an impish smile. If he could make her smile, they'd be okay. He was sure of it. Kind of sure.

"I—"

"Robin, there you are." Mason walked up to them.

Jay couldn't help himself, he glared at the man. Lousy timing, buddy.

"Dad has a wedding surprise for Lillian that

I'm hoping you'd help me coordinate," Mason said while standing there in his precisely pressed slacks and collared knit shirt and loafers.

Who wore leather loafers at the beach?

"Of course I will." Robin smiled at Mason.

Sure, go ahead. Smile at the guy. It's not like we're in the middle of my apologizing or anything.

"Great, I'd appreciate that." Mason nodded to him. "Hey, Jay."

"Mason." He turned to Robin. "I better get back to the kitchen."

"We'll talk later, okay?"

"Nah, we're good. Don't worry about it." He turned and stalked back to the kitchen in a worse mood than before.

Robin headed back to the bungalow late afternoon for some paperwork she'd forgotten to grab this morning on her way to work. She walked up to the porch and saw her neighbor, Mrs. Gleason, sitting on her porch with her dog, Barney. She headed over to say hi.

"Hi, Mrs. Gleason, how are you and Barney doing today?"

"Not very good, dear." Mrs. Gleason

reached down and petted her dog. "You see, my daughter wants me to move into a retirement place."

"Oh?"

"Yes, and I understand. I do need more help these days and my daughter is always running over here to help me. I don't like being a burden to her."

"I can understand." Robin reached down to pet the beagle, then leaned against the railing.

"But there's a big problem." Sadness lingered in Mrs. Gleason's eyes, and Robin wasn't sure her neighbor hadn't been crying.

"What's that?" She asked gently.

"The retirement place my daughter wants me to move to—and it's right near her home on the mainland, so it's very convenient for her—they don't allow pets."

"Oh, no. Can you find a different place?"

"That's the nearest one to my daughter, and she already does so much for me. I had a little accident, and she doesn't want me driving anymore."

Robin had seen Mrs. Gleason's car after the accident and it didn't look like it had been such a little one, but thank goodness Mrs. Gleason hadn't been hurt.

"I've been trying to find a good home for Barney, but I've not had a lot of luck. My daughter said we could turn him over to the beagle rescue group, but… well, I can't bear to think of him with strangers, just some random people they pick. And Barney will miss me. I'm sure he will. The whole thing is breaking my heart."

"I'm sure it is. I'm so sorry."

"And my daughter is coming to pick me up soon. I'm going to her place for the weekend and my grandson is allergic to dogs, so Barney can't go with me. And Barney hates the kennel. We're dropping him off on our way. I feel like I'm just letting him down."

"I could take him for the weekend." She surprised herself by even offering.

"You could?"

"Of course. That's no problem."

Mrs. Gleason stood and gave her a hug. "You're a godsend, my dear."

"Let's get his things and bring him to my house. We'll get him all settled before I head back to work."

Mrs. Gleason looked down at Barney. "What do you say, boy? Want to spend the weekend with Robin?"

Barney just stared at Robin. She wasn't sure he was up for their newly concocted plan. She hadn't had a dog since she was a young girl. With Charlotte gone so much with Ben, she'd enjoy having Barney for a few days.

They got the dog's things and took them to her house, then Mrs. Gleason's daughter came by to pick her up. Robin and Barney stood on the porch, watching her pull away. "Come on, Barney. I still need to find those papers and get back to work."

Barney just sat there on the porch.

"Barney. Inside."

And yet, the dog just sat and stared at her.

She finally reached down and grabbed his collar and led him inside, where he promptly sat by the door. She went to the kitchen, hoping she'd left the papers there. After shuffling through a few stacks, she found what she was looking for and headed back to the main room.

Barney lay on the floor by the door, chewing on one of her red shoes. "Barney, give that to me." She took the shoe away from the dog and looked at it. Ruined. Completely ruined. "No. Bad boy. You don't chew shoes."

Maybe this whole weekend visit wasn't such a brilliant idea.

She went around the house picking up everything she could think of that Barney might get into. She firmly closed the doors to her bedroom and Charlotte's. She should really text Char and let her know that Barney was here, too.

Once she got the house all dog-proofed and made sure he had water in his bowl, she walked back to the main room and found him lazing on the couch. Okay, sure, we let dogs on the couch here, right?

"I've got to go to work. But I'll be back soon."

Barney looked up at her with bored eyes.

"Okay, then. You be good." She walked back outside, locking the door behind her. As she glanced back at the house, Barney was peeking out the window, watching her leave. She waved to him, which seemed kind of silly, but she did it anyway.

CHAPTER 7

C harlotte walked into the inn that afternoon. Her sister had texted and said they were here. This was the first time they'd visited since Charlotte had finally stood up for herself with them. She and her father had worked out a comfortable truce, but things still weren't working out very well in her relationship with her mother and her sister.

After Charlotte ran out of all her excuses for delaying—like cleaning all her paint brushes and rearranging the paint colors along with unloading the dishwasher and scrubbing the counters—she'd finally gone over to meet them for happy hour.

She found them sitting outside on the deck. "Hi." Her mother and sister were dressed in freshly ironed slacks with not a wrinkle in sight and rather fancy blouses. Not appropriate for beachwear, but then they always seemed overdressed. She looked down at her simple skirt, t-shirt, and sandals. Her father—remarkably—was in khaki shorts and a knit shirt instead of his standard country club attire he usually wore to casual affairs. He looked relaxed and at ease.

Her father rose and gave her a quick hug. Her mother didn't. Nor did Eva. Her mother did nod with a small smile, though. Maybe that was progress.

"I'd forgotten how horrible the humidity is down here." Eva looked up from where she was doing something on her phone. "I don't know how you can stand it."

She didn't answer Eva's complaint and perched on a chair beside her dad, ready to flee if needed.

"I was going to order you a drink, but I wasn't sure what you'd want," her father said and grinned. "Except I'm quite clear these days that you don't like chardonnay."

She smiled back at him. "I think I'll have a beer."

He signaled the waiter and looked at her mom and Eva. "You two ready for a refill?"

"I'll have a *chardonnay*," Eva said.

"I think I'll switch and have a martini." Her mom handed her empty wineglass to the waiter.

Her dad ordered the drinks, and she sat there fiddling with her bracelet, waiting for the right opportunity to tell her family about her wedding date. Neither her mother nor her sister had asked to see her engagement ring. There hadn't been much excitement when she'd called to tell them about the engagement.

Her father leaned close. "Let me see that ring of yours."

She held out her hand, glad someone in her family was interested.

"That's very pretty." He nodded.

Her mother looked at it next and frowned a bit. Eva glanced at it and said, "Kind of small, isn't it?"

"It's perfect." Charlotte snatched her hand back and then gratefully took her beer from the waiter. She took a sip, then set it down. "And I have news. Ben and I have set our wedding date. The first weekend in December."

"Fabulous." Her father smiled.

"*This* December? That's not enough time to

plan a wedding." Her mother looked over with shock plastered on her face.

"It's enough time for me. I'll have everything planned and ready."

"You can't get married then. That's such a busy time of the year. We have business functions almost every weekend." Eva shook her head.

"And you know I run the annual Snow Gala. That's the second weekend in December. I couldn't possibly get away the weekend before that."

"You just need to change the date," Eva said. "You need to be considerate of your family's time and obligations. We're not as… *free* and *uncommitted* as you are. Our lives are very busy."

She counted to ten, which she always seemed to need to do when her family was around. Then she took a sip of beer. "We've already picked the date and scheduled the wedding for here at the inn. I reserved a suite for you here from Thursday of that week through the weekend. Let me know if you're not coming and I'll cancel the reservation."

Eva raised her eyebrows. "You're going to

keep that date after Mother and I said how inconvenient it was?"

"I am."

"We'll be there." Her father reached over and patted her hand. "Wouldn't miss it for the world."

"But, Glen, you know it will be impossible for me to get away the weekend before the Snow Gala."

"You'll just have to figure out a way, Isadora. I, for one, am very excited and happy for you, Charlotte."

And he was probably right. He was the only one. She looked up and saw Ben headed their way. She jumped up, crossed over, and hugged him, holding tightly for a moment before letting him go. "Thanks for coming. I thought you might not be able to get away."

"I wasn't going to just leave you to have all the fun." He grinned and gave her a quick kiss.

"Fun, right, that's just how I was thinking tonight was going." She took his hand and led him over to her family.

Her father stood, and the men shook hands.

"Hello, Benjamin," her mother said. But without much warmth or enthusiasm.

"Ben, what's this absurd idea about getting

married at Christmastime? We were just explaining to Charlotte how difficult it would be for us to get away then." Eva shook her head, her curls bouncing around, framing her face. She gave Ben a charming smile and a wink. "You'll change it, right?"

Was Eva actually *flirting* with her own sister's fiancé?

"Ah… well…" He looked at her questioningly.

"No, we're still on for the first weekend in December." She nodded to him, imploring him with her eyes to not encourage any more discussion about changing the date.

"Oh, good." He smiled at her and squeezed her hand in solidarity.

"And we'll all be there." Her father sat down and took a sip of his drink, then looked at her mother and sister. "All of us."

She gave her father a wide smile as Ben sat down next to her. She was really liking this new, supportive version of her father. Liking it a lot.

She wasn't sure if she'd ever work things out with her mother and sister, though. And she might just be a horrible person because sometimes, *just sometimes*, she wasn't sure if she cared if she did.

ROBIN WAS busy the rest of the afternoon and evening at the inn. She kept glancing at her watch, hoping Barney was doing okay alone at the bungalow. He wasn't left alone very often, as near as she could tell. Mrs. Gleason usually brought him along when she did her errands. She had noticed that Mrs. Gleason was walking to do her shopping these days. She should have offered to drive her to the store but hadn't put two and two together that Mrs. Gleason wasn't driving anymore. Some neighbor she was.

She glanced around the empty dining room. It had been a busy night here. And though she usually dropped by the kitchen to check on things before she left, she didn't really have time to do that tonight. Besides, Jay was being weird. Okay, he'd apologized, and she was sure they'd get back on better footing, but she needed to get home to Barney and was too tired to try and work things out with Jay.

She hurried down the sidewalk—walking home alone and convincing herself she didn't miss walking home with Jay—and saw lights on in the bungalow as she got there which reminded her she'd forgotten to text Charlotte about Barney. She opened the door and stood still, looking around in amazement. Shredded paper covered the floor, and another chewed up shoe mocked her from the middle of the room. Where in the world had he found that? The pillows from the couch were scattered all around on the floor. She leaned down and snatched up the shoe. At this rate, she'd be barefoot by the end of the weekend.

Charlotte walked into the room with Barney trotting by her side. "Is there something you forgot to tell me?"

"Char, I'm sorry. Mrs. Gleason was going to the mainland for the weekend to stay at her daughter's and needed a place for Barney to stay and I offered. Did you know she's moving to a retirement place?"

"I did. She hasn't been driving since her accident and her daughter wants her closer to her." Charlotte bent down and petted Barney, who sat innocently at her feet.

"I must just be clueless. I didn't notice she wasn't driving. Just thought she was getting a lot of walking exercise these days." She leaned down and started picking up the shredded paper. "I thought I had the place dog proofed. Guess not. Did he get into any of your things?"

"Nope."

"He just must have a thing about my shoes." She held up the tattered sandal Barney had chewed on. "Maybe I'll start a new trend of chewed up shoes. It will be all the rage real soon now."

Charlotte grinned. "All the rage, I'm sure."

"I'll make sure everything is out of Barney's reach before I head to work tomorrow."

"Good plan."

"So, how did drinks with your family go?" She reached and gathered up the throw pillows on the floor and placed them back on the couch.

"It was… interesting. Thank goodness Ben got away from the marina early and came by. Eva insisted I change the date of our wedding because it was inconvenient for them. They are busy and important, you know."

"Ah, your sister. Never changes, does she? So, are you going to move the wedding?" Her mind raced through other possible dates that might be open for a wedding at the inn.

"Not a chance." Charlotte shook her head. "If anything, it makes me more determined to keep the date and make the wedding perfect."

"That's my girl." She turned to look at Barney. "And you. No more eating shoes."

73

Barney just looked at her with soulful, innocent eyes.

JAY KEPT WATCHING the kitchen door, thinking Robin would make her usual check-in before she headed home. He wanted to suggest they walk home together and maybe he could mend fences with her after that Mason guy had butted into their conversation earlier today.

He turned when he heard the kitchen door swing open, but it was Lillian. "Everything go okay with dinner tonight?"

"Right as rain." At least he wasn't screwing up his cooking. Just his life.

"Good. Where's Dana?"

"Sent her home. I'm just cleaning up the last of the dinner mess and getting a few things prepped for breakfast."

"You do know that you're supposed to be letting her—I don't know—assist you? That's usually what assistant cooks do…"

"I am." But he knew he barely was.

"Try to let her do more."

"Lil, I'm not leaving if that's what you're

worried about." He hooked the skillet he was holding on the rack above him.

"I'm not worried, though you'd have every right to. You're making quite a name for yourself."

"On this tiny island."

"Don't sell yourself short. Have you read the reviews for the inn? All of them rave about how great the food is here."

"Really?" He narrowed his eyes. "It's just... plain cooking. A lot of it is my grandma's recipes."

"There is nothing plain about your cooking. It's flavorful and varied, and you've turned this dining room around. I'll always be grateful I found you."

His heart swelled in his chest, filled with gratitude. "I'm the one who's grateful. Really, Lil. You taking a chance on me? Best thing that ever happened to me."

Lil walked over and rested her hand on his. "Jay, you just needed to believe in yourself. And you told me you didn't do what they said you did. I chose to believe you. And you haven't proven me wrong. Life isn't always fair to us. Sometimes we just need to make peace with our past and move on." She looked directly at him.

"I hope you can make peace with yours sometime."

He didn't know about making peace with his past, but he did know that he'd never let Lillian down. She was the first person—since his grandma—who'd ever believed in him without question. And he'd never forget that.

"Plus, you're a wonderful chef. And I count you as a friend, too." She smiled at him, turned, and left the kitchen.

He'd never met someone quite like Lillian. Somehow, her calling him a friend made everything even better. He'd just sort things out with Robin, and his world would fall back into place again. He needed that.

He turned to finish up his work. Maybe he would let Dana help out more. He really should… What could it hurt?

CHAPTER 8

T he next morning Robin gathered her courage and went to check on things in the kitchen at the inn. She wanted to smooth things over with Jay. The awkwardness between them was silly. He'd been in a bad mood, apologized, and they could just move forward.

And Charlotte had been wrong about Jay, anyway. There was nothing between them.

Although, she would be watching him with new eyes to see if she saw any signs of... *anything*. But, no, that was ridiculous.

Dana looked up and smiled at her as she entered the kitchen. "Morning."

"Good morning, Dana. How goes things in the kitchen today?"

"Great."

She looked around the room. "Where's Jay?"

"He headed to the mainland to the open market to pick up fresh produce. He wasn't impressed with the produce our regular supplier had this week and said the open market always has great items."

So much for talking things out with him this morning. "I know he's picky about his ingredients."

"He is. But he's such a great chef. I'm learning a lot from him." Dana paused, looked down at the dough she'd been kneading, then back at her. "I just wish he'd let me do more. Give me more responsibility. I'm trying to take over more. Show Jay I can do things. About the only thing he lets me make without looking over my shoulder at my every move is this sourdough bread."

"Jay is a bit… possessive with his kitchen."

Dana grinned. "A bit?"

"Okay, a lot. But both Lillian and I have talked to him about giving you more responsibility."

"You have?" Her eyes lit up. "You think I'm ready for more?"

"She does. I do. And you are."

Dana let out a long sigh. "If only Jay believed that."

"I'll talk to him again. I think he should start giving you at least one dinner a week and one lunch to plan and be in charge of."

"That would be wonderful."

"I'll talk to him." Robin turned and left the kitchen. She would talk to Jay about Dana. She just wasn't sure he'd listen to her.

She went about her busy day at the inn. They were completely booked this weekend, and she still had a few things she needed to check on regarding Lillian's wedding next weekend. And she'd told Lillian to take next week off to concentrate on the wedding, but she was fairly sure Lillian wouldn't listen to her any more than Jay.

She managed to find time to run back to the bungalow and check on Barney. This time she found he'd chewed up the book she'd been reading. At least it wasn't another pair of shoes, but now she'd have to get the book again to find out the ending. She put all books up out of reach and returned to the inn.

Sara walked into her office early that evening. "You ready to go?"

Robin glanced at the clock. "Is it six already?"

"It is. Time to go."

"It's nice that Charlotte's father invited us to Magic Cafe for dinner tonight, but I feel like I'm so behind on everything. And I feel badly leaving Mrs. Gleason's pup alone."

"I just texted with Char to let her know we're headed out and she said she'd just let the dog out and she was leaving, too."

"Oh, good."

"And I'm sure we won't be very late tonight."

Robin stood and stretched. "I was going to go home and change clothes before dinner, too."

"You look fine," Sara assured her.

They headed outside and down the sidewalk to Magic Cafe. Tally greeted them when they arrived.

"Hello, girls. Charlotte and her family are already here. They have a table over at the side by the fans. I tried to give them that big table by the sand so they'd have a better view, but her sister insisted on the other table."

"Eva doesn't like the humidity and heat down here." Robin shrugged. "Actually, I'm not sure there's much of anything she likes about Belle Island."

They joined Charlotte and her family.

"Mr. Duncan, it was so nice of you to ask us to join you." Sara slid into a seat.

That left the only open seat, the one next to Eva, for her. She slipped into the chair. "Hey, Eva."

"Robin." Eva bobbed her head and her perfect curls danced across her shoulders. She gave Robin a once-over look and Robin could tell she'd failed miserably in Eva's estimation.

She tugged her own hair back—a bit frizzy from the humidity—and wished she'd had time to go home and change. The Duncans—Mr. and Mrs. and Eva—were all dressed in what could only be called country club casual. Charlotte, though, was in one of her fabulous bohemian style outfits. The type of outfit Charlotte loved, and Mrs. Duncan hated.

"I'm glad you two could join us. The three of you used to be inseparable growing up. I thought it would be nice to see you together again." Mr. Duncan waved to the waitress. "A bottle of champagne for the table. We'll celebrate my daughter's upcoming wedding."

Charlotte leaned forward. "I let Barney out

before I came. He's doing fine. Nothing destroyed."

"You mean since I checked on him this afternoon and he ate my novel?"

Charlotte laughed. "I guess since then. He does seem to like to destroy your things."

"You two have a dog?" Eva frowned.

"We're just dog-sitting for a neighbor," Robin explained.

"Dogs are just so... messy." Eva rolled her eyes.

She wondered how many times Eva would roll her eyes at them tonight.

"Barney's a good dog. He just... chews things." She didn't know why she was defending the dog. The dog obviously had a thing about her possessions.

She didn't miss that Charlotte smothered a grin.

The waiter poured champagne for all of them, and Mr. Duncan raised his glass. "To Charlotte. May her Christmas wedding turn out just the way she wants it."

Eva rolled her eyes—that was number two—barely lifted her glass and certainly didn't clink with anyone. Mrs. Duncan politely smiled...

that kind of polite smile that a person knows is really fake. But Robin and Sara enthusiastically clinked glasses with Charlotte and Mr. Duncan.

"To our Char," Robin said.

"Charlotte," Mrs. Duncan said.

Robin wasn't sure whether Charlotte's mom was actually toasting or correcting her for shortening Charlotte's name to Char…

The dinner went on… and on. Eva kept making snide remarks and was up to five eye rolls at last count. Mrs. Duncan's stony look of disapproval never left her face, and Mr. Duncan tried hard to smooth things over. Charlotte wavered between quiet, mad, and forced jovial. She gave Charlotte a supportive smile from across the table. Charlotte raised her buttered roll in appreciation.

"How many rolls is that Charlotte? You'll need to watch your weight now. Once you pick out a wedding gown, you can't balloon up." Mrs. Duncan shook her head. "I assume you'll come to Austin to find a dress. I'll take you to the best shops in the city. Oh, and I'll get together a list of people you must absolutely invite. Business associates and people like that. Though, with the ridiculous choice of time of year, who knows how many will be able to come."

Sara put a hand on Charlotte's arm. "I think Charlotte is planning on a small, simple wedding, right Char? Just family and a few close friends."

"What will I tell our friends? Your father's business partners?" Mrs. Duncan pinned Charlotte with an incredulous look.

"That I'm having a small, family and close friends wedding?" Charlotte shrugged.

"Really, Charlotte, could you be more difficult? First the impossible choice of wedding dates and now you won't even let mother invite any of her friends?"

"I think a small wedding is nice. More intimate. More romantic," Robin chimed in, trying to throw in her support.

"Maybe we can all just come and wear swimsuits and flip-flops." Eva shook her head *and* rolled her eyes. Number six... or was it seven?

"How about another round of drinks?" Mr. Duncan interrupted.

"That sounds great, Dad." Charlotte turned to her mother. "I'm going to plan the wedding I've dreamed of. Every detail just like I want.

On the day I want. You and Eva can come… or not. I'd love to have you there, but if it's too inconvenient, okay. And I'm not coming to Austin to look for a dress. I'm looking on the mainland or I've thought about having Ruby make one for me. She did such a wonderful job on Sara's."

"Sara had a couture dress made?" Eva raised an eyebrow.

"A friend of Lillian's remade my mother's wedding dress for me to wear," Sara said.

"So a homemade wedding dress? Like someone would make in home ec? Do people even do that anymore?" Eva frowned.

"Oh, look, here comes the waiter." Robin smiled widely as the server came over. "Let's get more drinks like Mr. Duncan suggested." She gave Charlotte a hard look, hoping her friend would just let it go. It didn't pay to argue with Eva.

Charlotte ignored her look. "It wasn't homemade… not that there's anything wrong with that. It was a *custom* dress. And it was beautiful."

"Whatever, Charlotte. You always do what you want, anyway." Eva shook her head with her perfect curls and leaned toward her mother. "What do you say we get some martinis?"

"I think that might help." Mrs. Duncan nodded with one last look of disapproval sent in Charlotte's direction.

CHAPTER 9

Charlotte, Robin, and Sara walked out of Magic Cafe and Robin sucked in a deep breath of air. She didn't know how Charlotte could handle meals with her family. They were —oppressive. She gave her friend a hug. "Well, the good thing is, they leave at the end of the weekend."

"Easy for you to say. You don't have to see them again tomorrow. They want to take Ben and me to dinner. Again. They're going to scare Ben off."

"Ben doesn't scare easily, and I thought you said that Ben and your Dad get along well now."

"Pretty good, thank goodness. So we only have to deal with Mom and Eva." Charlotte sighed. "I'm going to head to the marina for a bit and see Ben. You going to go check on things at the inn?"

"No, I better go home and see how Barney is doing."

"That's probably a good idea. You don't want to lose another pair of shoes now, do you?" Charlotte's eyes twinkled.

"He's a bit of a rascal, isn't he?"

"At least with your stuff."

They headed out and Charlotte turned off to the marina and Sara turned off to head home. Robin slowly wandered down the sidewalk, enjoying the evening.

Poor Charlotte. Her family still was impossible, and she was fairly certain neither Mrs. Duncan nor Eva would ever approve of anything Charlotte did. Eva had made it clear— over and over—how inconvenient the date of Char's wedding was.

She debated popping in for an ice cream at the Cone Corner but decided she better get back to Barney. She turned onto Palm Street and ran into Jay. Literally.

"Oops." He reached out to steady her. "You okay?"

"Sure. I guess I was looking too closely at

the Cone Corner, trying to decide if I needed an ice cream cone to top off my dinner."

"Let's get one." Jay suggested, his eyes hopeful.

Her resolve faded. "Let's."

They went into the shop, and she ordered a double scoop of butter pecan and Jay ordered vanilla. Plain vanilla. They walked back outside.

"You headed home? I'll walk with you," he offered, sounding much nicer than he had the last few days.

"I am." She nodded. It's not like she could stop him from walking the same direction she was headed. Not that she wanted to stop him. They ambled on, making small talk about the weather and nothing about their disagreement or whatever it was. She climbed up the stairs of her porch when she got home and turned around to face him.

"Jay, I—"

"Hey, Robs—"

They laughed. "You go first," Jay said.

"You," she countered.

Jay took the last bite of his cone, shoved his hands in his pockets, and looked at her. "I don't like it when we're not getting along. I'm sorry I've been such a beast. A creep. A jerk."

"An ogre, a scoundrel, a miscreant… Go on, I won't stop you." She grinned.

He gave her a wry smile. "Anyway, I've missed you. I miss you popping in and talking to me. I miss you swiping cookies." His mouth curved into a wide, lazy grin. "And I even miss teasing you. So can we put this all behind us?"

"Please, yes, let's. I've missed you, too."

A relieved look crossed his face. "Great. It's back to teasing you, then."

"And I'm back to swiping cookies."

A bark sounded from inside.

"What's that?" Jay asked.

"That's Barney. Mrs. Gleason's dog. I'm dog sitting for the weekend. He must have heard us talking."

"Well, we should probably let him out for a bit, don't you think?"

She unlocked the door, and Barney stood there looking at her with an annoyed look. He sauntered past her, paused and looked at Jay, and wagged his tail. Jay reached down and petted him. "Good boy."

She glanced into the bungalow. Not so good boy. The pillows were all on the floor again.

They stood and let Barney do his business, then the three of them headed inside.

"Get you a beer?" She asked as she dropped her purse near the door. On second thought, she placed it up on a shelf way out of Barney's reach.

"Sounds good."

She brought him a beer and a big glass of ice water for herself. Jay had settled on the couch with Barney lying beside him with his chin propped up on Jay's leg.

"Looks like you've found a friend." She reached down and picked up a couple of throw pillows and settled them on the couch and the overstuffed easy chair, then sank onto the chair. "I don't think Barney likes me much. He eats my shoes and chews up my books and throws the pillows on the floor."

"He's probably just bored and lonely being alone here, aren't you boy?" Jay stroked the dog's head.

"He doesn't get into Charlotte's things."

"Maybe she's better at putting her things away."

She took a sip of her water and set the glass on the end table, wondering if Barney would come over and tip it over if she left the room for the briefest second.

Jay glanced over at her while she sat there.

And glanced again. What was up with that? Which of course made her think about what Charlotte had said about him. That he liked her. But he never gave any sign at all that he did. He'd never asked her out. No, Charlotte was crazy.

Jay stretched out his long legs, careful not to disturb Barney. "So, I've decided to give Dana more responsibility at the inn. I think she's ready for it." His forehead creased. "I hope so anyway. I'm going to let her be in charge of a dinner this week. Besides, I'm really busy getting food ready for Lil's wedding."

"I think that's smart. I think she's ready to do more. Be responsible for more." Ha, she hadn't even had to bring up the subject. Now if he just actually did what he said he was going to do.

"What was Mason's dad's surprise for Lillian?" Jay asked as he sat and mindlessly petted the dog. Barney closed his eyes.

"I can't say because, you know, it's a surprise. But I'm helping Mason with it."

She didn't miss the slight frown on Jay's face when she mentioned Mason. "Anyway, Gary is very thoughtful and I think he'll make Lillian very happy. That's what counts."

"It is." He smiled. "I guess I should head out." He gingerly got up, trying not to disturb the dog, and took a last swallow of his beer.

She stood, eyed Barney, and picked up her glass as she led Jay to the door.

He turned to her and briefly rested his hand on her wrist. "I'm glad we smoothed things out between us."

A wave of heat smoldered through her. She looked down at where he had touched her and tried to gather her thoughts, her words. "Uh, me, too."

Jay slipped out the door, and she stood there staring at her wrist. Charlotte couldn't be right, could she? Was there something between them? Though she hadn't seen him have any reaction to touching her. She shook her head. Charlotte was just messing up her thoughts.

She turned to look at Barney—who had already knocked two pillows onto the floor.

JAY WALKED BACK to his home, staring at his hand off and on as he walked. He'd felt a bolt of electricity surge through him when he'd touched her wrist. What's that about? He'd touched her before. Hugged her a few times. Touched her arm to get her attention.

So why was tonight's touch so... powerful?

He'd almost jerked his hand back in shock. Which was crazy, of course.

But he'd seen her eyes light up at his touch. He was certain of it. Positive. Almost certain.

Maybe.

He inhaled a deep breath of the fresh salty air and let it out slowly. Maybe things were more complicated than he'd originally thought.

CHAPTER 10

R obin stood at the kitchen door the next
evening at the end of her workday. She'd
had to stop herself from popping in there about
a million times today. She'd walk up to the door,
but then turn and walk away. She and Jay had
made a tentative peace last night, and she didn't
want to break it. If she walked in there and he
was cold to her again... well, she hadn't wanted
to face that.

She took a deep breath, gathered up her
courage, and finally slipped into the kitchen—
first time for the whole day. She looked around
and saw Dana putting things away and cleaning
up the kitchen. No sign of Jay.

"Hi, Dana. Did dinner go well?"

Dana turned to her and smiled. "It did.

Jay's pot pie was a big hit." She put down the towel she was holding. "And thank you for talking to him. He's letting me plan the lunch menu and be in charge of the lunch at the end of the week so he can work on Lillian's wedding prep."

"I'm glad he's letting you do that. Baby steps. Though I kinda think it's a big step for him." She grinned. "So where's Jay? Did he leave already?" *Was he avoiding her?*

"No, Lillian asked him to put tonight's cash payments in the safe. I expect him back any moment."

She couldn't decide if she should hang around and wait for him because it was just supposed to be a casual drop-in visit. Not a hunt-him-down visit. Or maybe she was just avoiding him, afraid to see that disinterested cool look in his eyes again.

The door swung open and Jay strode in. He stopped abruptly when he saw her. She held her breath…

And his face broke into a casual smile. "So, you came to swipe a cookie, I assume?"

"Of course. I hear there were oatmeal cookies tonight."

"I saved you some." He walked over and

reached into a cabinet and took out a plate of cookies. "Go ahead."

She reached for a cookie and took a bite. "I swear, you make the best cookies."

"Old family recipe. Same as the pot pie. Though we had some extra veggies I threw in the pie tonight. Can't stand to waste any food."

He glanced around the kitchen, taking in every detail, as she was used to him doing. Scanning, looking for anything that needed to be done or put away. He turned back to her. "You headed home?"

"I am." She held her breath. Again.

"Mind if I walk with you?"

"That would be nice." She let out her breath.

He turned to Dana. "You'll lock up when you're finished?"

"Yes, I've got this."

"Okay, see you tomorrow."

They headed out the back door, out of the heat of the kitchen, and out into the warm night air that was still cooler than the kitchen. They walked in silence for a bit, which wasn't that strange. They often walked in companionable silence. She just didn't know if tonight the silence was companionable or awkward…

"Another ice cream tonight?" he asked.

"I don't think so. The cookie was enough dessert."

They walked under a lamplight and she glanced at him and found he was looking at her. Almost staring. She gave him a little smile and quickly glanced away, pretending she hadn't noticed he was watching her. They walked the rest of the way to her bungalow and stopped at her porch steps.

"Thanks for walking me home."

"You going to let Barney out?"

"Yes, I should."

"How about we take him for a walk? He'd probably like that after being cooped up all day."

"That's a great idea." They went inside and she found the leash. She called Barney, but he didn't come.

"Barney, wanna go for a walk?" Jay called out. The dog came trotting up to them.

"Here, he obviously adores you." She handed Jay the leash, and they headed outside and down the sidewalk.

"Should be a full moon by Lillian's wedding next weekend." She scrambled for small talk, not wanting to continue with their silence.

"That will be nice. I heard Charlotte talk all about something called fairy lights for the deck. She threw around words like fireflies and magical." He shook his head. "But no doubt, knowing Charlotte, she's got the decorations all planned for Lillian."

"She does. I'm sure it will be magical."

They slowed their pace as Barney stopped to explore a group of bushes. Exciting stuff, those bushes. They stood under the streetlamp and let Barney nose around. Jay turned to her, and she could see a look in his eyes that took her breath away. Literally. He reached out and took her hand. "Robs, I'm glad we talked."

Breathe, breathe, breathe.

"I waited all day for you to stop by the kitchen. I finally thought that maybe my apology hadn't gone so well. Or that you were still afraid I was in a lousy mood." His voice was low, soothing, mesmerizing.

Take a breath or you'll pass out. She slowly inhaled the thick salty air.

"I'm glad you came by tonight." His eyes glimmered like summer lightning. "And I was wondering… speaking of Lillian's wedding. Would you… I mean, since we're both going…

would you like to go with me? I know we both have to kind of work, but…"

And just like that, the moment was shattered. Yes, she'd love to go with him. No, she couldn't, because she already told Mason she'd go with him…

"Oh, Jay… I… uh…" *Nice. Put your words together.* "Mason asked me to go with him. I mean, I'll be busy doing some work stuff and making sure things go smoothly, and he is his dad's best man so he'll be busy, too. But…"

"No, that's fine. I'll be busy making sure everything with the food goes well. I just thought—never mind."

His eyes shuttered, closing off the glittering look she'd seen just moments before.

With another gulp of the sea air, she gathered her courage and reached out to touch his arm. A shock swept through her and she swore his eyes smoldered at her touch.

"But I'd rather be going with you. I just said yes to him to be… nice. He doesn't know anyone here."

Jay nodded, then stared down where her hand rested on his arm. He pulled his gaze from her touch and looked directly into her eyes, into her soul.

For that brief moment, they were totally connected.

She held her breath—*yet again*—and wondered if he was going to kiss her. She *wanted* him to kiss her. He *was* going to kiss her. She was certain. Pretty certain. And how long could she hold her breath...? Thoughts ping-ponged through her mind.

He leaned toward her slightly.

Finally, *finally*, he *was* going to kiss her.

Barney barked at a rabbit hopping out of the bushes and tugged on the leash, pulling Jay along with him, the moment shattered with the incessant barking. She swore that dog had it in for her.

CHAPTER 11

They headed back to Robin's bungalow, the silence deafening between them. When they got to her porch, he unleashed Barney, who sat on the top step looking at them, turning his head from one to the other.

The light from her front window bathed her in a golden circle. Jay considered kissing her… like he was going to back there on the sidewalk before Barney started barking like a fool. But the moment was gone now. Or quite possibly he'd lost his nerve.

She stood looking at him. Waiting. Watching. Her hair blew in the breeze with a few locks framing her face, and she rested one delicate hand on the railing.

Details. He was into all the little details

again.

With a snap decision, he took a step forward. "I was thinking."

"Yes?" Her eyes widened in anticipation.

"Let's go to Lighthouse Point for a picnic tomorrow. We could go after breakfast but be back in time for the dinner rush. Dana can handle it. You're always saying to let her handle a meal."

"I… uh…" A confused look covered her face, but she recovered quickly. "I think I could get away. For a little bit, anyway. That sounds like fun."

"Perfect. I'll pack us a lunch. You could come by the kitchen midmorning?"

"Okay, I'll see you then." She looked at Barney. "Come on, Barney, let's go in."

The dog just sat there staring at her.

"Barney, go inside." The dog looked at him, stood, stretched, and padded inside the house.

Robin rolled her eyes. "He never listens to me." With that, she slipped inside.

He took the long way home, hoping the cooling air would soothe the fire inside him. Something had stirred inside of him at her touch. Something he'd been ignoring for a long time.

But it was hard to ignore anymore. He had feelings for Robin. He'd had them for a long time but just couldn't admit it to himself. But after tonight... it would be ridiculous to try to lie to himself.

And the Mason guy. Grrrr. Why did he always get in the way? Even if she had said she'd rather be going with him to the wedding—you know, if he'd thought to ask her earlier before Mason had gotten around to it.

At least he'd asked her to go on a picnic with him. Nothing formal or a date, but just a picnic out at the point. Kind of like when he'd planned on asking her to Classic Movie Night at the park, but Mason had ruined that, too.

But Mason couldn't possibly ruin their picnic tomorrow—could he?

He scowled as he walked into his house, closed the door, and leaned against it. The room mocked him with its sparse furnishings, so in contrast to Robin's cheerful, homey bungalow. A bungalow that she was in right this very minute. The sparseness of his house didn't usually bother him, but tonight the room seemed cold. Lonely. Empty.

He didn't even bother to turn on the lights and headed to his bedroom.

Robin sat on her bed long after Jay had gone. She wished Charlotte were here to talk to. She needed to talk through her thoughts, through her feelings.

She'd been almost certain that Jay was going to kiss her right there under the lamplight. And she'd wanted him to. After all these years, the secure just-friends footing she had with him had shifted. Everything she thought she knew about the two of them had changed.

If only Barney hadn't barked...

Then again, for just a moment, she'd been certain Jay was going to kiss her there on her front porch. When he said he wanted to ask her something, she thought he might ask her if he could kiss her. But, no, it had been to ask her on a picnic.

A picnic was fun.

But it wasn't a kiss.

And she longed for Jay to kiss her now. Longed to feel his lips on hers. And wanted to know if they'd feel an instant connection...

... or if they were better off just being friends.

CHAPTER 12

J ay got up early the next morning determined to get to the inn before Dana. It was almost starting to annoy him that she often got there before him. Besides, he had lots to do and wanted to make a special lunch for the picnic with Robin. He was kind of holding his breath on that, hoping something didn't come up to stop them.

He reached for the handle on the back door to the kitchen and noticed it was unlocked. He couldn't help the sigh that escaped. Dana beat him again.

A logical person, a good head chef, would come up with a schedule that they shared so they weren't both working all the time…

He strode inside. "Morning, Dana." He saw she had cinnamon rolls started and walked over to look at them. She glanced at him with a look in her eyes like she was afraid he'd tell her they weren't good enough. "Those look good."

Her eyes widened, and a slow grin crossed her face. "Thanks."

"Oh, and you're in charge of lunch today. You good with that? I'm going out for a while."

Her eyes grew even wider. "Yes, of course I am. That's great." She nodded enthusiastically.

"Good."

He hurried about with his morning chores. Getting the coffee going, pulling things from the fridge, making up pancake batter. The breakfast rush kept him busy until midmorning when he stopped to make the picnic lunch. He made sandwiches using some of Dana's fresh sourdough bread. He washed strawberries and put them in a container. Robin loved strawberries. He sliced some cheese and packed up some crackers, then made some sweet tea and poured it into a thermos. At the last minute he grabbed a few of the oatmeal cookies. Then he tossed in an apple and an orange.

Probably way too much food but, honestly,

he knew nothing about picnics. He'd never been on one and wasn't sure what had prompted him to choose a picnic for an outing with Robin. It had just popped into his mind and he'd asked her.

He turned to find Robin standing beside him. "Feeding an army?"

He grinned. "I couldn't decide so I put in anything I thought of. You ready to go?"

She frowned. "I'm sorry—"

He swore if Mason had gotten in the way of this picnic…

"I need another twenty minutes or so. Is that okay?"

He broke into a wide grin. "Yep, sure is." She wasn't canceling. She just needed more time. "I'll swing by your office in twenty."

"Perfect."

Yes, it was perfect. They were going on a picnic. He and Robin. Today.

ROBIN SLIPPED into shorts and a t-shirt, finished up the ordering she needed to do online, then waited for Jay. She looked up to see him standing in the doorway to her office. He had on shorts and a t-shirt with the picnic basket in one hand, a beach blanket tucked under his arm, and that irresistible lazy smile on his face.

She jumped up from her desk. "I'm all ready."

"Come on then. Daylight's burning."

They headed out to the beach and slowly walked to Lighthouse Point. Large fluffy clouds dotted the sky, and the sun darted in and out from behind them. A strong breeze blew in from the water, tossing her hair about, and she reached in her pocket for an elastic and pulled her hair back in a ponytail. They walked along the water's edge, and she stopped to pick up a shell.

Jay laughed, opened the picnic basket, and pulled out a small bag. "Here, I knew you'd be shelling as we walked. You just can't resist the call of the shells, can you?"

She grinned and dropped the shell in the bag, reaching to pick up another shell that she just had to have, then they continued down the beach.

The golden light highlighted Jay's cheeks, and the breeze ruffled his hair in a wild and carefree manner. His long, tanned legs stretched out as they walked, but as usual he slowed his pace so she could keep up with him. He was always thoughtful like that.

They settled on the blanket at the point, and she leaned back on her elbows, watching the birds dart around at the water's edge, playing a merry game of chase. She welcomed this unaccustomed break to her routine.

Jay seemed relaxed today, and she saw no sign of the intensity she'd seen in his eyes last night. Or had she only imagined it?

Robin looked over at him and then quickly at the sandwiches he was unwrapping. The crust was perfectly brown, the bread perfectly baked, and she knew this probably irritated Jay because he'd grudgingly admitted to her that Dana made better sourdough than he did.

She sat up and took the sandwich he offered her. She briefly chanced a glance over at him again and caught him staring at her. She quickly looked back at the food spread before her and reached for a glass of the sweet tea. The cool liquid did nothing to soothe her jangled nerves. She grabbed a napkin and waved it in front of her face, hoping it would cool her flushed face, but it just fluttered ineffectually.

She didn't know why this day with Jay was

any different from any other day she'd been around him. She spent hours and hours with him in the kitchen, walking home from work, or just hanging out. So why was this different?

But she had to admit it *was* different. At least to her. Something had subtly changed between them. She felt electricity crackle all around them as if waiting for a storm coming in from the sea.

And she was certain he felt the same thing. Almost certain. Unless she was wrong…

To her, at least, it felt like they were racing in front of the storm, trying to reach shore before it hit. Yet knowing they weren't going to make it in time. Knowing the storm would crash over them.

She turned and looked at him again, and this time she didn't turn away from his gaze. Their eyes locked, and she held her breath.

He reached his hand over, covered hers, and squeezed it lightly. "We're in some kind of pickle now aren't we, Robs?"

"What do you mean?" Only she knew exactly what he meant. She just wasn't ready to admit that fact.

"You know what I mean. There's something here, isn't there? Something between us.

Something different." His voice was husky and insistent.

So he *did* feel it.

"There is something here, I'm just not sure what it is." She looked at him and saw the fire blazing in his eyes, just like last night. She hadn't imagined it. That exact look was right there in his eyes, yet again. She shivered slightly in spite of the heat of the day, in spite of the fire burning within her.

He slowly ran his hand up and down her arm, sending thrills of electricity surging through her.

His forehead creased. "It seems strange that after five years or so we're just sitting here discussing what this could be. We've been friends for a long time."

"We have, but something has moved, something has shifted. And I'm not sure I want it to change because what if everything blows up in our faces?" She looked out over the water, afraid of where the conversation was heading and yet wanting it to get there. She turned back to him, searching his face as if it held all the answers.

"You know, Robs, I think there's only one way to solve this."

"And what's that?" Her words came out in a breathless whisper, and she couldn't look away from his intense, fiery gaze.

"I think the only way to fix this is to kiss you. See what happens."

She could barely hear his words over the pounding of her heart and the crashing of the waves on the shore.

And if she didn't take a breath pretty soon she was going to faint. She inhaled deeply, her eyes never leaving his as he leaned closer to her and pressed a gentle kiss to her lips. Then he deepened the kiss, and her hand went up to grab his shoulder to steady herself and she swore that fireworks and lightning crackled and crashed around them.

He finally pulled back, stared at her, and let out a long, deep breath. "Wow, Robs. Why did I wait so long to do that?"

She reached up and touched her lips. "I don't know. Why did you?" She sent him a tiny smile, then glanced up at the sky, surprised to not see actual fireworks or lightning bolts.

"I don't know either, but I'd like to make up for lost time now." His eyes gleamed with purpose.

"That's a good plan."

He leaned in and kissed her again. And then kissed her off and on throughout their picnic. A picnic that was filled with laughter, and ease, and kisses. So many kisses.

CHAPTER 13

Jay was thoroughly enjoying himself. If this is what picnics were like, he wanted to go on one—with Robin—every day for the rest of his life. His heart was singing inside of him. Throbbing with life and joy. This was better than perfecting an absolutely flawless dish. And not much in his life could top that. Although Robin probably wouldn't be keen on being compared to cooking.

He stared at her, stretched out beside him. She was resting on her elbows and smiling slightly as she looked out at the waves.

The ringing of a phone caught his attention, and he glared at his cell sitting on the blanket where he'd tossed it. The incessant ring was annoying. He didn't want to talk to anyone. He wanted to sit here and kiss Robin. He glanced at the number.

"It's the inn." He sighed and answered the phone. "Hello?" He practically growled into the phone.

Robin grinned at him and sat up, sipping innocently on her sweet tea with the glass pressed up to those lips of hers.

"What?" He frowned. "Okay, I'll be back as quickly as I can." He clicked off the phone. "Oven stopped working. It's been a little cranky lately, but I can usually get her to work. Dana's in a bit of a panic."

"We should go then." Robin jumped up and started collecting their things. They packed up the picnic basket and headed for Charming Inn, hand in hand. He liked the feel of her hand in his and the way she'd look up at him and smile as they walked along.

Her cheeks were rosy from the sunshine, and her lips were pink from the kisses. And all he could think was that he wanted to kiss her again.

"Oh, heck, Robs." He dropped the basket and pulled her into his arms and did kiss her again.

She grinned at him when he finally released

her. "Once you get started on something, you kind of like to keep going, don't you?"

"You bet." He nodded, picked up the basket, and they hurried the rest of the way back to the inn.

By some kind of unspoken mutual agreement, they dropped hands as they neared the inn. He wasn't ready to share this newfound relationship with Robin and certainly didn't want to talk to anyone about it... or have anyone gossip about it. He headed to the kitchen and she headed back to her office.

Dana looked like she was about to burst into tears when he strode into the kitchen.

"I'm sorry. I had everything under control. I did. But then the oven went out, and I used the old, smaller one, but things got backed up. And I know I need to get things started for dinner tonight, too. I'm sorry."

"Hey, not your fault. Let me see if I can make her work again." He got out some tools and messed with the connections on the stove. They really did need to get another backup oven. Or a new oven and this one could become their backup. He'd mention it to Robin and see if they had it in the budget.

"Did you get it?" Dana hovered close. "I am so sorry for ruining your time off."

"You didn't ruin it." Nothing could ruin it. He'd had a fabulous afternoon. "And look, the oven works again. Let's get the dinner prep going."

"You're not mad?"

"Mad? Why?"

"Because it's the first time you've left me in charge like this and I failed you."

"You didn't fail me. The oven kinda did. But it looks like you did fine. Lunch crowd is over and all's well."

He turned away but didn't miss the relieved look on Dana's face. Was he really that horrible a boss to work for? He pursed his lips. Maybe he had been. He should be giving her more of a chance. He could remember when he was an eager assistant, wanting to learn more and do more. He was going to remember to be more patient with her and give her more responsibility.

Heck, he felt like being nice and patient with everyone today. He smiled and whistled while he got to work on the dinner prep.

~

LILLIAN REACHED for her phone and saw it was Etta Swenson calling from the historical society. "Etta, good evening."

"Lil, I hope I'm not bothering you. I know you're busy getting ready for your wedding."

"Of course, you're not bothering me."

"I was doing some research, and I found some information that might lead us to figuring out the owner of the journal you found."

"You did?"

"I looked up the census records, and I found two possible leads for who the author might be. In the 1880 census there was a John Smith with a wife, Matilda and daughter Anna. The ages work out about right for your Anna. The 1890 census was destroyed. But there's still a John Smith listed in 1900 census, but no wife, no children. Living alone. I assume Jane was born after 1880 and both girls had moved out by 1900."

"Really? Well, that gives us something to go on, doesn't it?"

"So I did some searching on the cemetery records and there was a Matilda Smith who died in 1886, beloved wife of John Smith and mother to Anna and Clara."

"So this John Smith was raising the girls on his own?"

"I'm not sure. There was a Belle family living next door to them. But no Jane Belle listed. But with the 1890 census missing, she might have been born after 1880 and moved out by 1900. Possibly. At least this is a start. I printed all this out for you."

"Thanks, Etta. After the wedding I want to start looking into this more. And I really appreciate your help."

"Okay, I'll help in any way I can. Night, Lil."

"Night, Etta." Lil hung up her phone, went in to her bedroom, and picked up the piece of turquoise sea glass they'd found with the journal. She rolled it over in her palm, wondering why it was hidden with the journal. Wondering about the mysterious Anna. Wondering what happened to her. She really wanted to find answers. She sighed as she set the sea glass back on her night table. For now, she needed to just concentrate on her wedding. After things settled back down, she was determined to solve the journal mystery.

She went back to the kitchen to make some

chamomile tea before heading to bed. Her hip was beginning to ache a bit like it did when a storm was coming in.

CHAPTER 14

On Monday Robin went to the mainland again to find a dress for Lillian's wedding—and this time she brought Charlotte. Mrs. Gleason was back home and had taken Barney, so at least she didn't have to worry about what damage he was doing at the bungalow while they were shopping.

Charlotte pulled out three dresses at the first shop they went into. "Try these on."

Robin tried on the first one and loved it. It was very her and comfortable and made her feel… what? Pretty? And she sheepishly wanted to look pretty for Jay… even if she was going to the wedding with Mason. What a mess she'd made of things.

Charlotte frowned and looked at her.

"What's wrong. You said you loved the dress, but your face says something different."

She turned to her friend. "Oh, I love the dress. It's just... Mason asked me to be his date at the wedding."

"Okay, and that's a problem why?"

She sank onto the seat beside Charlotte. She hadn't found the right time to talk to Charlotte about Jay. About what had happened. She'd been keeping it to herself. Taking the memory out like a special keepsake and looking at it over and over. But now she felt the need to talk. She glanced around, then leaned close to Char.

"Because Jay kissed me yesterday." A small smile tugged at her lips. "He kissed me a lot."

Charlotte broke into a wide grin. "Well, it's about time."

"And he asked me to go to Lillian's wedding. But I'd already said I'd be Mason's date."

Charlotte's forehead creased, and she nodded. "Yep, you have a problem."

"Though I'm just going with Mason as a date since he doesn't know anyone in town. There's nothing serious going on there."

"Yet, Jay is going to be jealous." Charlotte's eyebrow raised.

She let out a long sigh. "I know he is. But I

can't do anything about that now. It just is what it is."

"You could always explain things to Mason…"

"Tell him what? That Jay kissed me and my heart swooped to the sky and all I want is to spend more time with him and for him to kiss me again?"

Charlotte laughed. "Something like that. But maybe not so detailed."

"I don't know. I already told him I'd go with him. It will be okay, won't it?"

Charlotte shrugged. "I don't know…"

She jumped up. "Anyway, I love this dress. We're finished here."

"Try on the other two before you decide." Charlotte nodded toward the dressing rooms.

"But I love this one." She ran her hands down the fabric.

"Go."

Robin came back out with the second dress on. She loved it, too. "How do you do this? Pick out the perfect dress? I was in this store last week and found nothing."

"Now the third." Charlotte motioned with her hand. "Try it on."

She came back out with the third dress.

"How am I ever going to decide? I love them all." She turned around slowly to show Charlotte.

Charlotte's forehead creased as she looked at Robin. "I think—if you really don't have a preference—that I like the second one the best on you."

"Perfect, because I love all of them and I'd never be able to make a decision."

"It goes well with your eyes and I think we'll pull your hair up for the wedding. I'll do a fancy knot or something for you."

"I don't know what we'd do without you, our very own fashion coordinator."

She put her clothes back on, bought dress number two, and they headed outside. "Look, there's the wedding shop. As long as we're here, let's pop in there and you can look at wedding dresses." She pointed at the shop across the street.

"I don't know…"

"Got to start looking soon." Robin grabbed Charlotte's hand. "Come on."

"Okay, I'll go to the shop. But then we'll grab lunch and you're going to tell me everything about Jay and what happened."

They went into the shop, and Charlotte

looked through the dresses on display. "I don't really see anything that looks exactly like what I'm looking for."

"How about that one you looked at three times? Over there?" She pointed to a dress on a mannequin.

"I guess I could try it on."

A worker got the dress for Charlotte and she tried it on. She stood in front of the three-way mirror. The simple dress draped from one shoulder and accentuated Charlotte's slender waist.

"Oh, Charlotte, you look beautiful." Her friend looked like someone from a bride's magazine, but then Charlotte always did make clothes look gorgeous on her.

Charlotte turned this way and that. "It's a beautiful dress... but it's just not what I've imagined."

The shop worker brought Charlotte another dress, and another. After the fifth dress she tried on, she shook her head. "Enough. Nothing is quite right."

They thanked the worker for her help and left the store. "So, do you want to hit another shop? There's another wedding shop in the next town."

"I don't think so. It's like I can see the dress in my head, but I'm not seeing it in the shops. Or online for that matter."

Charlotte did have her own style. Robin could see how the classic wedding dress varieties wouldn't work for her. She looked at Charlotte and grinned. "We could always wear swimsuits and flip-flops like Eva suggested."

"Very funny."

"Why don't you see if Ruby can make you what you have in your head? Explain it to her and maybe she could draw it up and make it?"

"I think I will ask her. I just want everything to be perfect. And I have plenty of time… just not *lots* of extra time."

"Perfect, we'll go talk to Ruby."

"If she has time and if she wants to do it."

"Lillian said Ruby loved redoing the dress for Sara and look what a great job she's doing with Lil's dress. I bet she'll say yes." Robin had a good feeling about this. She just knew that Ruby could make Charlotte the perfect dress for her wedding.

They walked back outside into the sunshine, and Charlotte pointed to a restaurant down the street. "It's time. We'll go there and you'll talk and I'll listen."

Robin nodded. Maybe if she talked with Charlotte, she'd be able to figure things out herself. So much had changed with just a few kisses—make that *lots* of kisses.

ROBIN HEADED TO THE KITCHEN—JUST to check on things, of course—as soon as she got back to the inn. Jay was busy working by the counter, his back to her. She looked at his broad shoulders and his inevitable t-shirt stretched across his back. His head was bent, concentrating on whatever it was he was working on.

She crossed the room and touched his arm. He turned to her, and his face broke into a wide grin.

"Hey, you." His voice was low and warm, and she swore it made her tingle.

She was hopeless.

She smiled back at him. "Hey, yourself."

"Come to swipe cookies?" His eyes sparkled, teasing her.

"No, I'm stuffed. Went to lunch with Char after we went dress shopping. Finally found a dress to wear to Lillian's wedding."

A brief look of disappointment crossed Jay's

eyes at the mention of the wedding, but he quickly hid it. "Well, that's good."

She reached out and touched his hand. Lightning zipped through her.

Perhaps that was a mistake.

"Jay, I'm sorry I told Mason I'd be his date. I didn't know that... *this*... was going to happen."

"Not a problem. I'll be busy at the wedding, anyway." His smile and his eyes didn't quite confirm that it wasn't a problem.

"Robin, there you are."

She turned to find Lillian standing beside them, her forehead creased in worry.

"You needed me?"

"I was wondering if you took the cash deposit to the bank."

"No, I locked it in the safe to take it when I headed out this morning but it was gone so I figured you took it."

Lillian frowned. "No, I didn't." She turned to Jay. "You put it in the safe this weekend, didn't you?"

Robin looked at Jay and saw the color drain from his face until he was ashen.

"I did. Just like you asked. And I made sure the safe was locked when I left," he said defensively.

Lillian looked at Jay for a moment. "I was just checking. I was sure you did."

"But it's missing now?" Jay cocked his head to one side.

"It is."

Dana dropped a pan to the floor, and they all whirled around at the sound.

"Sorry." She reached down and picked up the pan and turned back to her work, but it was obvious she'd heard the conversation.

"I don't know what to make of it." Lillian frowned. "There's just the three of us with access."

"Lil, I didn't take your money." Jay stiffened, his eyes dark and icy cold.

Robin stared at him in surprise. Of course Jay hadn't taken any money. Lillian would never think that. She turned to look at Lil.

"I didn't think you did, Jay." Lillian reached out and put a hand on his shoulder. "You'd never do that. I know."

Jay looked relieved—slightly—but still stood frozen with a small vein beating on the side of his forehead.

"Maybe I misplaced it? I've been so scattered this last week." Lil frowned. "But I don't think I did. I'm always careful with the deposit. I guess I'll call Sheriff Dave. I'm not sure what else to do. It's an old safe. Came with the inn. Probably not that hard to break into, and I've had the same combination forever." Lillian sighed. "And it did look like some of the papers in there were shuffled around."

"You really think someone broke into the safe?" Robin sucked in a sharp, quick breath.

"I don't know what else could have happened." Lillian frowned and turned to leave. "I'll go make that call."

Jay stood there with an empty expression on his face, his jaw clenched, and one hand balled into a fist, watching Lil walk away.

"You okay?" Robin asked, trying to figure out what was going on with the looks between Lillian and Jay.

"I'm fine. Just fine." The deeply etched frown on his face proved he was *not* fine.

"You don't look it."

"I said I'm fine." His voice was sharp. "I should get back to work." He turned from her and started methodically chopping and dicing the vegetables on the counter.

Okay, then. Back to being cold and distant. So maybe it wasn't such a big deal that she was going to the wedding with Mason after all.

She stalked out of the kitchen. Jay was the most confusing, exasperating, bewildering, puzzling man she'd ever met. And she threw in baffling, complicated, perplexing, and unfathomable for good measure.

CHAPTER 15

Robin left the kitchen and headed off to find Lillian and see what she could do to help. She couldn't imagine anyone stealing from Lil. Just couldn't picture it. Lil was the kindest soul she'd ever met.

Lillian was nowhere to be found, so she headed for her office and pulled out her notebook of events. She pulled up the weather forecast for this weekend and frowned. When had they changed the forecast? Now it looked like a storm was headed their way. A big storm. That was not what Lillian needed on her wedding day.

It could still be wrong. Florida weather was unpredictable at best. She should make sure the backup plans were in place, though, just in case.

They'd use the tent if it was just slightly rainy and they'd clear out the lobby and reception area if it really stormed. The reception could be moved into the dining room instead of having the buffet outside. She quickly jotted some notes, then got up to find Lil. She really should know about the possible changes to her wedding plans.

She scoured the inn, then finally went to The Nest and knocked.

"Come in, it's open." Lillian called out.

She found Lillian sitting in her favorite chair, knitting.

Lillian looked up. "I'm a little stressed. Usually knitting will help calm me down. The repetitive motion, the colors weaving through the piece." She set down her knitting. "But it's not working today."

"I'm sorry about the missing cash."

Lil sighed. "I know. I keep thinking it will turn up. Like did I take it out to bring it to the bank and forget I did that? I am a bit scattered with all the wedding plans."

"You've been a bit—less organized—but that doesn't seem like you to misplace the cash deposit, or not even remember taking it out of the safe."

Robin paused, then plunged on in. "Speaking of wedding plans. There's a chance that the weather might turn a bit stormy this weekend."

"Really?" Lillian shrugged. "That can't be helped, either. The weather will be what it will be."

"I'm making the backup plans for if we need them. I'm sorry, though. I know you wanted the ceremony and reception outside. Maybe we can still make that happen."

"I did want it outside, but the location isn't the important part of a wedding."

Lillian was nothing but practical at all times.

"We can wait until later in the week to make the call."

Lillian nodded.

"Did you get a hold of Sheriff Dave?"

"I did. He'll be here later this afternoon."

"Do you know why Jay was so upset when you were talking to us about the cash?"

Lillian's eyes turned guarded. "No, was he?"

Lillian was one sharp cookie, and she had to have known that Jay was upset, but Robin didn't question her further. "I'll go get the backup plan in place."

"Thank you. I'll follow you back to the inn

139

in a moment. I need to get back to work since knitting is doing nothing to settle me down. Wedding jitters, I guess, plus this missing cash."

JAY LOOKED up from where he was pounding chicken breasts—with a little too much force— to find the sheriff standing at the counter. He caught his breath but forced a smile.

"Jay."

"Sheriff Dave." He nodded at the man and set down the mallet. Didn't pay to be flaunting a mallet when a person talked to a sheriff.

"I wanted to ask you a few questions."

Of course he did. "Ask away."

"So there's only three people who know the combination to the safe." The sheriff opened his pad of paper and poised his pen over it.

"I guess." He glanced over to where Dana was working and trying to pretend she wasn't hearing the conversation. There was no privacy in the kitchen, so anyone here could hear what was said.

"And you put the cash in the safe this weekend like Lillian requested."

"Yes." He walked over to the sink and ran

the water, scrubbing his hands, then drying them.

The sheriff followed him. "And that's the last time you saw the cash?"

"Yes." He gritted his teeth, annoyed that his heart was racing and he could feel his blood pulsing in his veins. Here he was being interrogated. Again.

"I just had to ask because... well... your past."

"So are you accusing me of something there?" He whirled around to face the man.

"No..." The sheriff scribbled some notes. "Just getting the facts." He looked at Jay. "For now."

"If that's all, I need to get back to work."

"I'll probably have more questions later." The sheriff turned and left the kitchen.

Jay sagged against the counter. His past was never going to leave him alone. Never.

CHAPTER 16

Jay contemplated telling Robin about his past. He'd never mentioned it in the five years he'd been here on the island… and neither had Lillian. But he was afraid it would all come out now. It would be better if Robin heard it from him than from the town gossiping about him. Someone was sure to find out, and then the news would spread like hurricane winds through the town.

He turned to Dana. "I've got to go do something. You got everything you need for a bit?"

"I do. Do you need me to run dinner tonight? I can, you know."

"No, I'll be back soon. But thanks." He turned to go find Robin.

And find her he did.

In the lobby.

Laughing with Mason.

Perfect, just perfect. He turned to leave, but heard Robin call out his name. Inhaling a deep breath, he turned back, crossed the lobby area, and went over to Robin and Mason.

"So, Robin tells me the wedding might have to be moved inside," Mason said.

News to him. And why wouldn't Robin have mentioned it to him? He was only in charge of all the food for the wedding. Might be helpful if he knew where they were serving it. He cocked his head and looked at Robin. "Is that true?"

"Yes, I was coming to tell you." She almost looked guilty.

"A piece of information that might be good for me to know," he said dryly.

"I'm getting all the backup plans in place, just in case." Robin rushed her words. "But, of course, I was going to consult you so we had all the reception plans worked out too."

"Of course." He eyed her.

"Mason was just here because we're finalizing the surprise for Lillian."

"That's nice." Did they detect the sarcasm in his voice? Here he'd come to tell her the truth, but really, did she need to know? She seemed interested enough in this Mason guy. They'd been laughing and Mason had his hand on her arm while they were talking.

Maybe his own thinking had everything twisted with Robin. He'd thought something had started between them... but Mason probably didn't have a past like his. Maybe he and Robin were really just destined to be friends. And maybe that would be best for Robin.

This whole cash fiasco had thrown him off. Made him unsure of himself, and he hated feeling like his world was tilting out of control.

"I should go get dinner ready. Let me know what you want done about the reception food." He turned away, not looking back even once, and headed back to the kitchen.

Robin frowned and watched Jay walk away. He was upset, that much was clear. Whether it was because she was here talking to Mason or from whatever was going on between Jay and Lillian, she wasn't sure. But ever since Lillian had asked about the cash, he'd been the cold and distant Jay that she'd come to abhor.

She turned back to Mason. "Sorry, now what were you saying?"

"I arranged for a limo to pick them up after the reception. We have the company plane ready to fly them to that small Caribbean island. Dad made the reservation for the hilltop villa. It overlooks the sea and has one of those small infinity pools. They'll have a chef who brings their meals, but I'm having it stocked with other foods, wine, and beer."

She couldn't quite fathom having a private jet at her disposal or being taken to a small Caribbean island. Or a private chef, for that matter. But she was all for Lillian having a week of pampering.

"I'm sure Lillian will love it all."

"Dad said he would surprise her the day of the wedding. He just told her to pack for warm weather for their honeymoon."

"I love seeing someone spoiling Lillian. She's always there for everyone else. It's time she found someone to love her and spoil her."

"Thanks for your help with this. I wasn't up on limo companies or even what airport to have the plane waiting at."

"Glad I could help." She turned at the sound of someone calling her name. Sara and Noah came walking up. Noah's niece, Zoe, followed them, pulling a large suitcase.

"Hey Mason, Robin. Oh, Mason, do you know Zoe?" Sara asked.

Mason nodded. "I think we met at Sara and Noah's wedding."

"We did." Zoe smiled. "Though that day is kind of a whirlwind of memories."

"Zoe is going to stay at Charming Inn. I told her that was unnecessary. She should stay with us. But she insisted, saying we were newlyweds." Sara shook her head. "I keep telling her we still have her room at the house, just like she left it."

"I'll stay next time, I promise. You two just need your space for a bit," Zoe insisted.

Zoe turned to Mason. "Are you staying here?"

"I'm actually moving to the inn today. Dad's rental is up on the cottage. So he's getting a room here, too, until after the wedding."

"You are?" Robin turned to him, surprised.

"It was kind of a last-minute decision. Dad was going to renew his lease for another month, but it seemed pointless since he'll move in with

147

Lillian after they get back from the honeymoon. My stuff is out in the car."

"Let me get you both checked in."

Sara and Noah headed out to run errands, and Robin checked in Zoe and Mason, giving them rooms on the top floor with great views. They headed up the stairway with their bags.

She turned to go back to her office. She wasn't ready to face Jay and his mood right now. She finished up in her office and went to work the dinner shift, but still didn't enter the kitchen.

Mason showed up for dinner and she sat him at a table by the window. Alone. She did feel bad about that. "How's this?"

"It's nice." He sat down and took the menu.

She noticed Zoe standing at the entrance to the dining room. "Say, if Zoe is eating alone, would you mind if I sat her with you? It gets kind of lonely eating alone."

"Sure, that would be fine." He nodded.

She crossed over to Zoe. "You here alone?"

"I am. Sara and Noah were still busy running errands and I'm famished."

"I can seat you with Mason."

Mason waved from across the room.

"That would be nice. I eat alone so often back home."

She led Zoe to Mason's table, and she slipped into the chair across from him. It must have been a good decision because every time she looked over at Mason and Zoe they were talking and laughing. There, now Mason knew two people in town. Well, Zoe was from out of town, but she was here now for the wedding.

The dining room finally emptied and she grabbed the last of the dirty dishes off of a table and headed to the kitchen, determined to talk to Jay and find out what was going on.

The kitchen was empty except for Dana.

"Jay gone?"

"Yes, he left a while ago. Said he had somewhere to be. He's leaving me in charge more often now. I like it." Dana smiled.

Jay had left. No walking home together tonight. No talking. Disappointment swept through her. She'd had just one day of magic with Jay.

One day.

Now, everything was gone, shattered, and she didn't know why.

CHAPTER 17

Jay sat nursing a beer at the Lucky Duck. He mindlessly munched on the nuts in the bowl in front of him. This day sure hadn't ended like he thought it would. And he'd been a coward to duck out early tonight. He just didn't know how he was going to explain everything to Robin. Explain his past. And he didn't want to see the disappointment in her eyes when he told her. She might not even believe the truth. Not many people did. Except his grandma and Lillian.

"There you are. You're not answering my texts. Thought I might find you here." Ben slid on the stool beside him.

"Didn't feel like talking."

"You kidding me? You finally go out with Robin and now you don't want to talk about it?"

"I didn't go out. We just had a picnic."

"And you kissed her…"

How did… of course. Robin had told Charlotte who had told Ben. As far as he knew, the whole town knew by now. Not that it mattered. It was a one-time deal because everything was suddenly going to hell in a handbasket.

"It doesn't matter. And I don't want to talk about it."

"But—"

"Seriously, Ben. One more word about it and I'm outta here."

Ben held up his hands. "Okay, okay. So, what's this I hear about cash going missing from Lillian's. Who would do that?"

This conversation wasn't any better than talking about Robin. "I don't know who took it."

"It just seems so strange. You think someone could have broken into the safe?"

"I don't know."

"Lillian didn't need this the week of her wedding."

"No, she didn't." He took a sip of his beer,

hoping Ben would move on to yet a different subject.

"Charlotte said the sheriff was out asking questions."

"Mm-hmm."

"I hope they find who did it. Who steals cash from a place like Charming Inn?"

Ben was obviously not going to let this die, so he deftly changed the subject. "So, have you and Charlotte made any other wedding plans?"

"Not many. Her mom and sister don't like the date, but Charlotte hung firm on it, so we're still getting married at Christmas. She's going to talk to Ruby about making her wedding dress. That's about all I know. Though Charlotte has a big notebook going with ideas and things. I'm just saying yes to anything she wants."

"Good plan." Jay glanced at his watch. "I better head out. Long days this week getting everything ready for the wedding."

"I heard the weather might turn bad."

"Heard that. Let's hope not." He slid off the stool. "See you soon." He turned and headed out before Ben could bring up yet another subject he didn't want to think about, much less talk about.

MASON HAD SUGGESTED they take a walk on the beach after their dinner at the inn. Zoe thought that was a perfect idea. She always ate so much more when she came to the island than when she was back at home. But Jay's cooking was excellent, and she hadn't been able to resist his pot roast with a side of shaved brussels sprouts. Oh, and the sourdough rolls. Those were wonderful. Then, she'd had a big piece of chocolate cake with thick fudge icing. She wasn't even going to think about the calories. Maybe the walk would help even things out in the battle of calories in-calories out.

An almost-full moon shone down on them, illuminating the sand as they walked. "I've missed this. Being able to walk on the beach. Living inland certainly has its drawbacks, even if I do love my job there."

"Where do you live? I guess I don't even know that." He glanced at her.

"Up by Orlando."

"I live in Seattle."

"Right, like Gary."

"Dad hasn't been back to Seattle since he found this island." Mason grinned. "Not sure if he's ever coming back despite my attempts to talk him into taking back his position as CEO of the company."

"Sara said you were acting CEO now." Impressive for a man his age.

"For now. It's just temporary. But if Dad doesn't come back, I'm not sure what will happen." Mason shrugged. "I just want Dad to be happy, so whatever he decides I'll be fine with it."

"I'm sure it's a hard decision for him." They continued walking along, slowly. The wind barely stirred the air, and the water gently rolled to shore, as if mocking the forecast for severe storms approaching. They veered down to walk at the water's edge.

"So, Noah is your uncle, huh? You two close?" Mason asked as they strolled along.

"Close? Very. He raised me."

"He did?" Mason paused and looked at her.

"Yes, my parents died when I was very young. Noah jumped in, left everything behind —including Sara—and came to raise me. Long story, but Noah and Sara dated long ago when they lived in Boston, but there was a mix-up and Sara didn't know why he left. Noah took me to vacation on Belle Island once since Sara had always talked about how wonderful it was."

"It is a nice little town, isn't it?"

"We loved it here, and eventually Noah and I moved to Belle Island. Then Sara came back here to help Lillian with the inn when Lil had a bad fall. Sara and Uncle Noah found each other again." She smiled. "The rest is history."

"Seems like this island has a way of making people find each other and fall in love." His eyes sparkled with amusement.

"It does. I swear it's a magical place." She let out a long sigh. "I miss living here. But, you know, work."

"Ah, yes. Work." Mason matched her long sigh. "I need to head back to Seattle right after the wedding. No rest for the acting CEO."

She paused for a moment, debating asking her question, then plunged ahead. "So... the wedding. I was wondering. Would you want to go with me? I don't have a date and, well, I thought since you probably don't know many people here... but then, maybe you already have a date." Her words came out in a rush, and she already regretted them after seeing his expression. It was going to be a definite no, she could tell.

"I'm sorry. I made plans with Robin to go as her date. Though I know she'll be busy working and I have best man duties."

She frowned. "I thought Sara said Robin and Jay had finally started going out. I mean, it's been town knowledge for years that they both like each other."

"They do? Jay and Robin? And they're dating? She didn't say anything to me." Mason frowned.

"That's what Sara said."

"I don't know then. I guess I'll talk to her tomorrow. Maybe she just said yes because she felt sorry for me not knowing anyone."

She felt a little foolish now for asking him to go with her. Of course, he already had a date. He was successful, good-looking, and... well, charming. And Robin was... beautiful. And funny. And a bit older than she was, probably closer to Mason's age.

But she'd totally enjoyed herself tonight, and it had been a long time since she'd enjoyed the company of a man like she had tonight. Oh, well. She'd just go to the wedding alone. Not a big deal.

CHAPTER 18

R obin looked up when she heard a knock at her office door and saw Mason standing there. "Good morning, Mason."

"Morning." He stepped inside. "Got a minute?"

She didn't really, but she put down her pen and nodded.

"So... I heard something. Last night. I heard you and Jay are seeing each other."

Robin sighed. "It's... complicated." She didn't even know how to begin to explain the situation.

"But you said yes to going to the wedding with me."

"Things have changed. Kind of rapidly and unexpectedly."

"Listen, go to the wedding with Jay. That's fine. Don't worry about me. I know you said yes because I didn't know anyone else here. You were being friendly. Anyway, Zoe asked me to go with her. So, I'll say yes to her, and you can go with Jay and it all works out."

She gave him a little smile. "Okay. If that's what you want."

"Good, I don't want to be your pity date." He sent her an impish grin. "Oh, and thanks for sending Zoe over to eat dinner with me last night."

"So you two hit it off?"

"She's… nice. Interesting. Easy to talk to." He shrugged with a grin still on his face, his eyes twinkling. "Yes, I guess you could say we hit it off."

"That's good."

"I think I'll go see if I can find her now and see if she still wants to go to the wedding with me."

She gave him a weak smile. "Good plan."

He left her office, and she sat staring at the empty doorway.

Well, great. Now she had no date for the wedding.

"Look, look." Charlotte burst into Robin's office later that morning.

Robin set down her work, glad for the interruption. "Look at what?"

"I went to talk to Ruby yesterday afternoon after our wedding dress shopping failure. I explained to her what I had in my mind for a dress." Charlotte waved some pages around. "And she called me this morning to come and see these."

Robin got up and crossed around to the other side of the desk as Charlotte spread the papers out. "Char, those look so you."

"I know. They do. Ruby is a wizard with design." Charlotte stood there grinning. "I actually like both of these two designs. I just need to decide which one."

She looked at both the drawings. They would both look wonderful on Charlotte. "How are you going to pick?"

"I'm not sure. I'll just stare at both for a bit, I guess." Charlotte laughed. "I'm leaning toward this one, though." She pointed to one of the drawings. "I love the neckline and the touch of lace."

"I like that one. Well, I like *both* of them."

"These are so much better than anything I tried on at the shop or anything I've found online." Charlotte sank into a chair with a satisfied smile. "So, what's new with you? You were already asleep when I got home last night and gone before I got up."

"New? Let's see. I no longer have a date to the wedding. Mason is going with Zoe."

"Really?" Charlotte raised an eyebrow.

"Evidently they've really hit it off."

"I thought he was going with you."

"Well, he heard that Jay and I were seeing each other, so he said he'd go with Zoe. But now Jay is barely speaking to me, hence, the no date."

Charlotte frowned. "Ben said something is up with Jay, but he doesn't know what it is. He's super moody."

"I don't either. I've tried to talk to him. Guess I'll try again."

"Men say that women are complicated, but I think it's really men who are complicated." Charlotte shook her head.

"Well, Jay sure is."

Zoe sat out on the shore under a beach umbrella. It had been a long time since she'd had a beach day. She'd offered to help with wedding preparations, but Lillian had insisted things were under control and she should go enjoy the beach. It hadn't taken much convincing to heed Lillian's advice.

She stretched out on a lounge chair with her e-reader by her side along with a big cup of ice water. She'd slathered on sunscreen and plucked her sunglasses from atop her head and settled them on her face to block the glare on the water. She finally leaned back, relaxed. She was dying to get into the new book she'd bought in the Sweet River series.

She closed her eyes, enjoying the moment, inhaling the fresh, salty air. She sensed or felt a shadow move over her and opened her eyes. "Mason."

"Hey, Zoe." He plopped down on the wooden lounge chair next to her. "Great day for the beach."

"It is."

"Dad chased me away. I think I was making him crazy asking him to make too many decisions. You know, little ones. Like what he's wearing to his wedding in just a few days." Mason gave her a lazy, lopsided grin.

She liked his grin and his one dimple that made his grins look entirely too impish. Should a big shot CEO have an impish grin? Once she quit staring at his grin, she answered him. "Lillian sent me to the beach. Said she had everything under control."

"I guess there's nothing for us to do but enjoy the day here on the beach. Mind if I join you?"

"No, go ahead. I'd like the company."

Mason kicked off his sandals and swung his long legs out on the lounge chair. He was wearing a practical outfit today with shorts and a t-shirt in contrast to his snappier attire she was used to. She liked this more casual version. He leaned back and laced his fingers behind his head, elbows up, watching a young boy and girl chase each other down near the water. A small smile played at the corners of his mouth.

The little girl screamed, and a young woman called out. "Don't tease your sister."

Zoe laughed. "I guess that's just what brothers do. Tease their sisters. Not that I have any siblings."

"Me, neither. Always wanted a brother, but

by the time I was old enough to know what was going on, my parents were barely speaking to each other. It was like they lived separate lives. They divorced when I was young."

"I'm sorry, that must have been tough."

"Not so bad. Never knew any better. Wasn't that close to either of them, really. They were always working. But I started working at Dad's company right out of college. Learned a ton from him."

"So you two are close?"

A frown crossed his features. "Not really. We do seem to be getting closer. Working together on CEO things. He's helped me a lot since I took over. I can see how this job could just suck all your time and energy." He shrugged. "I'm trying not to let it. But I do put in long hours trying to keep things running smoothly while Dad is gone."

She couldn't imagine running a big company at such a young age. Talking to the board of directors and commanding respect. She was just a lower executive at her job.

"I see you brought your reader with you. Hope I'm not interrupting."

"I always have a book with me. Either my

reader or I read on my phone. Do you read much?"

"Some. Used to read more before this whole CEO thing."

"What kind of books do you read?"

"Thrillers, a bit of mystery, some nonfiction." He looked at her. "And you?"

"Romance, women's fiction, mystery, legal thrillers—but nothing gory—a lot of genres."

"Movies?" He cocked his head to one side."

"I don't go to movies often, but I love to binge-watch series on Netflix and other video streaming services."

"Favorite color?"

"What's with all the questions?" She smiled at him.

"I figured I'd like to get to know my date to the wedding. If you're still free. And if you still want to go with me."

Her heart fluttered. *Silly heart.* "What about Robin?"

"Released her from her commitment so she could go with that Jay guy."

"I'd love to go with you." She might have to rethink the dress she'd brought to wear, though that was silly. It was a perfectly good dress. But she could still look for a new one...

"Perfect. I have best man responsibilities, but I'll catch you after the ceremony?"

"That sounds perfect." It did sound perfect. She was glad to have a date for the wedding. Not that she minded going alone. Kind of. Weddings always seemed a bit awkward to her without a date, which was silly. Seems there were a lot of silly thoughts going on now.

CHAPTER 19

By Wednesday Robin was afraid the coming storm was going to be a bad one. Fortunately for the wedding, it was a slow-moving storm, so it wasn't supposed to hit until next Wednesday or so. And for now, it was predicted to hit quite a bit north of the island. But with the possibility the tropical storm could even turn into a hurricane, there were so many preparations that needed to be done to the inn, just in case. Hurricanes were always unpredictable.

Technically hurricane season started June first, but it was rare to have an actual storm hit this early. Now, added onto all the wedding prep was storm preparations.

They were already getting room cancellations for next week. Many hotels and rentals only gave refunds of deposits if an evacuation was called for, but Lillian had always refunded guests' money if they didn't feel comfortable with a storm predicted to hit the area, even if evacuations weren't ordered.

But the wedding could go on as originally planned, outside like Lillian had wanted. She pulled out her notebook of events and scanned down the checklist of to-dos for the wedding. Julie from the Sweet Shoppe was doing the wedding cake and would deliver it on Saturday. The flowers were ordered, and the florist had called to confirm they'd be ready on Saturday, too.

Almost everything that could be done in advance was finished. There would be lots of work on Saturday to set up the chairs on the beach and the arbor and decorate for the reception.

Jay had the food all under control. Or she assumed he did. They hadn't said more than a few words this week, and Jay had been short and distant with her. She'd tried—twice—to get him to talk to her but hadn't had any luck. So now she was just giving him his space. She was finished trying to figure out Jay Turner. He could just stew in his bad mood.

She glanced at her watch and saw they were smack in the middle of the lunch crowd. She'd go check and see if they needed any help and chase Lillian away if she was in there. Lillian didn't quite seem to grasp the concept of taking this week off to prepare for her wedding.

She went to the dining room and spied Lillian headed into the kitchen. She hurried after her to tell her to go take a break and work on wedding things.

ABOUT THE ONLY GOOD thing to happen this week as far as Jay could tell was the fact that Mason and Zoe were spending a lot of time together. He saw them at dinner and walking on the beach and sitting out on the deck having drinks.

Much better than Mason lurking around Robin all the time. Much.

Not that it mattered anymore. Because he and Robin had hardly spoken this week. He just didn't know what to say to her now. He should explain things, but the longer he waited, the worse it got and the more strained things were between them. To her credit, she had tried a few times to talk to him, but it had never seemed to be the right time.

And he'd seen the look in her eyes as he shut her out. But it was really for her own good. She deserved someone much better than him. How had he ever thought he was a good fit with Robin? He wasn't even in her league, her universe. It had been one magical day at Lighthouse Point, and he'd remember it always. But one day was all it would ever be for them. Even if it was crushing his heart to know that. It was best for Robin, and that's what counted.

"Jay Turner? I need you to come with me for questioning."

Jay whirled around at the sound of Sheriff Dave's voice. The man stood there with a serious expression sculpted on his face.

"I thought you already asked questions." He dried off his hands on a towel and set it on the counter.

"I've got more."

He looked behind the sheriff and caught his

breath when he saw Lillian and Robin standing there listening. Perfect. Just perfect.

"Dave, what's this about?" Lillian took a step forward.

"I've checked into Jay's record. He went to prison and served time for this exact crime. Stealing from his employer. I need to bring him in and question him."

"Jay did not take my money."

Jay sent Lillian a grateful look.

"Maybe, maybe not. But I still have lots of questions for him."

"But he's getting the food ready for my wedding. Surely the questions can wait until later." Lillian came and stood by his side.

Robin still stood behind the sheriff with a dazed look on her face. Of course. She had no idea that he had a record. That he'd been sent to jail for stealing. He'd been lucky so far keeping that fact from the gossip on the island. Guess that was over now. And he was pretty sure the dazed and disbelieving look on Robin's face would haunt his dreams.

"I really need to talk to him. Now. It's always better to get as much information as possible, as soon as possible after an incident like this." Sheriff Dave drew himself up taller and put on an authoritative expression, though he did look slightly daunted by Lillian standing up to him.

Jay clenched a fist. He'd have no alibi this time, same as last time. He lived alone. No one could vouch for where he'd been the night the cash had gone missing.

"But—" Lillian started again.

"You need to let me do my job. If he wasn't involved, I'm sure we'll sort that out." The sheriff took a step forward. "Come with me, Jay."

Jay untied his apron and turned to Dana who was standing near them, her eyes wide. "Dana, I need you to take over the meal prep, but also the wedding prep. There's a list on my desk by the computer. Can you sort through it and keep going?"

"Me? You want me to work on the wedding food?"

"Yes, and the meals in the dining room." He turned to Lillian. "You'll get her more help if she needs it?"

"Of course." Lillian nodded.

He turned back to Dana. "It will be fine. You'll do fine. You're a very good chef. I believe in you. You can do this."

Dana's eyes glistened with tears. "I... I won't let you down."

He turned back to the sheriff. "Okay, let's go." He strode out of the kitchen with the sheriff by his side.

Robin still hadn't said a word, but he hadn't missed the hurt look in her eyes along with the confused expression on her face as he walked past her.

ROBIN WATCHED Jay and Sheriff Dave walk out of the kitchen. Deathly silence descended upon the room, and neither she nor Lillian nor Dana moved. She had no idea what was going on here. And what was that nonsense that the sheriff had said about Jay being in prison?

She slowly turned to Lillian, trying to gather her thoughts, so full of questions. Her heart felt like it was lodged in her throat and she swallowed before speaking. "Lillian, what's going on? What was that all about? He said Jay stole from his employer and has been in... jail?"

"It's not my story to tell." Lillian shrugged. "But I don't believe Jay ever stole from anyone.

And I'm positive he didn't steal from me. He wouldn't."

"But he went to jail for stealing?" She frowned.

"You really need to talk to him." Lillian turned to Dana. "Nothing said in here today leaves this room. Do you understand?"

Dana nodded.

"Now, Jay believes you can handle all this so I do, too. I'll make a few calls and get you more hands in here, though. But you'll be in charge."

"I... I can do this. I can." Dana looked at the door where Jay had disappeared. "Jay thinks I can handle this. He said he *believes* in me." She sounded astonished. "That means a lot to me."

"That's high praise from Jay. I'll get you more help, then I'm going to head to the sheriff's office and get this nonsense sorted all out." Lillian turned to Robin. "You've got things covered at the inn while I'm gone?"

"Of course." Though right now she didn't feel like she had anything covered, anything under control. What was going on?

Lillian left the kitchen and Robin stood watching Dana bustling around with Jay's list of to-dos in one hand. Dana would do fine.

Now she just had to worry about Jay. And

find out if all this was true, that he'd been in jail? Why had he never told her? And what else was he hiding from his past?

Her heart sunk and she felt so foolish. She'd thought she knew him so well, but no, she hadn't. She didn't know him at all.

CHAPTER 20

Lillian hurried to the sheriff's office. What a fine mess this was. She was positive Jay did not take the cash. She instinctively knew, the first time she met him, that he was not one to take anything from anyone. He was honest and honorable, even if he did keep to himself and tried to act all gruff and aloof. Underneath all that was a caring, giving, *honest* person.

She slid out of her car and walked toward the sheriff's office. She gritted her teeth at the sound of someone calling her name. Camille. Last thing she needed was Camille Montgomery right now. She ignored the call and kept walking.

Camille hurried up to her. "Lillian, didn't you hear me calling your name?"

"Hello, Camille." She stopped and swallowed a sigh.

"I saw the strangest thing awhile ago. I saw Sheriff Dave practically dragging your chef, Jay what's-his-name, into the office. What happened?"

"Nothing happened, Camille. Just a mix-up."

"I heard money was stolen from your safe."

Lillian grimaced. No secrets in this town.

"So did this Jay steal from you? I heard that it wasn't his first time. That he'd been in *jail* for stealing before. Didn't you check out his background before you hired him? You should always check out employee's backgrounds." Camille shook her head, her face a picture of disapproval.

Gee, thanks for the business advice. From a woman who'd never worked a day in her life… Lillian contemplated the best way to handle this and squash Camille from walking around town spreading rumors.

"Jay did not take any cash. That's ridiculous."

"How well do you know him?" Camille's eyes narrowed with suspicion.

"Camille, he's been working for me for over

five years. Five years. I know him well. He didn't take anything."

"I hope that Sheriff Dave can get to the truth. We can't have criminals just roaming freely around the island."

"He's not a criminal."

"He kind of is, right? He's been in jail." Camille flounced her hair behind her shoulder, and then leaned closer, lowering her voice. "I don't know that I even personally know anyone who's been to jail."

"Camille, I'm busy."

"Well, one more thing. I was wondering if my invitation to your little wedding was lost in the mail."

The invitation she hadn't sent because no way she was inviting Camille to her *little wedding*. "Oh, Camille, I'm sorry." But she wasn't. "We're just having a small, intimate wedding. Just family a handful of close friends."

"I'm hearing quite a bit of talk around town of people that are going," Camille accused her.

"No, not really. Just a few close friends," she insisted and then pinned the woman with a look she was fully aware Camille would ignore. "And don't go spreading rumors."

She turned and headed into the sheriff's

office with the sound of Camille's exasperated huff filling the air behind her.

JAY SAT across from the sheriff answering question after question. No, he didn't know where the money was. Yes, he'd put it in the safe. And yet again—no, he didn't know where the money was.

Sheriff Dave didn't believe him. That's the thing about having a record. No one ever believed you were innocent. Ever.

He turned at the sound of the door behind him opening, and welcome light streamed into the room.

Lillian.

Lillian looking like a whirlwind of energy and determination.

"Dave, time to drop this." She shut the door, and the room plunged into dim, depressing darkness again.

"I already told you. I need to question him. He's our prime suspect."

"He didn't take the money…" She paused, then looked at Jay. "And I'm so sorry to have wasted your time, Sheriff. But wouldn't you know? I went back and tore up my office and I found the cash. I'm so scattered this week, I must have taken it out and forgotten I did. I'm so sorry to trouble you."

"Oh…" The sheriff frowned. "Well, I guess that's good."

Jay didn't think good old Sheriff Dave actually thought it was good. The sheriff had been enjoying this tiny bit of crime on the island and seemed to relish this excuse to question him.

Jay stood up, his chair clattering behind him. He just managed to catch it before it crashed to the floor. "So, we're done here, right?" he asked. He'd had about enough of these questions and the sheriff's looks of disbelief.

"Uh… yes. I guess we're finished," the sheriff said. "And Lillian, I'm glad you found your money."

Lillian just nodded. "Come on, Jay. We have work to do."

He followed her outside, into the sunshine. The glorious sunshine. Pushing thoughts of the dim sheriff office's interior far from his mind. He faced Lil on the sidewalk. "Lillian, wait a minute."

"What?" Her face held an innocent expression, but he wasn't buying it.

"You lied to the sheriff. You didn't find the money, did you?"

"I did not." She shrugged. "But you didn't take it."

"But—"

"It was the quickest way to get the sheriff to leave you alone. He wasn't interested in tracking down who really took it. Anyway, no more talk about the money. I had a new safe put in with a new combination. And I'll give you the combination unless you don't want it. I'd understand if you don't, so something like this nonsense won't happen again."

"But now he won't look for who really stole the money."

"He wasn't anyway, was he? Doesn't matter. What matters is getting you back to the inn. Back to your life without the sheriff's preposterous questioning."

"Now that he knows my background he's going to question me more often about incidents that happen around town."

"Not if I have anything to say about it." Lillian's eyes flashed.

"Well, thank you."

"There's nothing to thank. You didn't take the money. Let's go." She turned and started walking to her car.

The woman never ceased to amaze him.

She paused and looked at him when they got to her car. "But there is one thing I need you to do."

"Anything." He sent her a grateful look, willing to do anything to pay her back for her kindness, yet again.

"Talk to Robin. Tell her the truth. You owe her that much."

Well, anything but *that*.

But he nodded. "I will."

CHAPTER 21

Robin didn't stop by the kitchen after the dinner crowd left, but that didn't surprise Jay much. She'd been noticeably absent after he'd returned from the sheriff's office.

Dana had worked on wedding prep and had everything going for dinner by the time he got back. She, thankfully, hadn't asked any questions upon his return.

But now the kitchen was cleaned and he'd run out of excuses to hang around, hoping Robin would stop by. He needed to go find her and talk to her. Explain things.

That's all Lillian had asked of him for all she'd done for him.

And Robin did deserve to know the truth. Then he'd leave her alone. Swing wide. Give her space. And quit worrying about who she dated. He scowled. Try to quit worrying about it, anyway, since it wasn't any of his business.

Maybe someday they could get back to being just friends, but he was certain things would never be the same. Ever.

He walked out into the night and headed to her bungalow. She opened the door after his one single knock and stood there silently just staring at him.

"Robs, can we talk?"

"I don't know. You haven't wanted to talk all week." Her eyes flashed.

He let out a long breath of air. "I know. I've been… distracted."

"So you call cold and distant *distracted* now?"

"Robs, please. Can we talk?"

She stepped outside and pulled the door closed behind her. "Out here." She settled onto a chair at the end of the porch, her arms crossed tightly across her.

He leaned against the railing, facing her, but not too close.

"I'm sorry for how I've been this week. I was just… things were just…" He scrubbed a hand over his face. "There are things I haven't told you."

"Obviously. That's quite an understatement."

"So what the sheriff said was true. I have been in jail. I was convicted of stealing cash at a restaurant I worked at." He searched her eyes looking for a reaction.

Her eyes were carefully cloaked, showing nothing.

"And I know everyone says this…" He still searched her face. "But I didn't do it."

One of her eyebrows raised, but she said nothing.

"I didn't. But I had no alibi and I had no money for a lawyer. I was convicted of stealing and went to jail. The only person in the world who believed I was innocent was my grandmother. She sat there in the courtroom and I could actually feel her heart breaking at the conviction. She got up, gave me a hug, and whispered she believed me."

Pain surged through him at the memory. His grandmother had been a proud woman, a fierce woman. She'd raised him when his own mother didn't have time for him. She'd taught him his love for cooking.

He looked away for a moment, collecting himself. "That was the last time I saw her. She died while I was in jail. When I got out, I was totally alone."

She sat for a moment, then spoke. "I'm sorry, Jay." Her voice was low.

He nodded. "I had a series of crummy minimum pay jobs. No one wanted to hire me because of my record. I finally got a job as an assistant cook at this fairly nice restaurant on the mainland. The chef treated me like dirt. Always threatening to fire me. Never letting me do anything, really. But at least it was a cooking job. Then the chef got sick and the manager let me do the cooking—he really had no choice—there was no one else." He crossed over and sat in the chair next to Robin.

Robin watched him closely but remained silent.

"Lillian happened to come to the restaurant that day. She enjoyed her meal—really enjoyed it—and asked to speak to the chef. Evidently the waiter said the real chef wasn't there and there was only me, this assistant cook. She still wanted to talk to me so the waiter came and got me. She asked if I was looking for a job. I said possibly but I'd have to explain some things to her first." He looked out into the darkness, remembering that day so clearly. "She came back at the end of my shift. I explained that I'd been in jail for stealing but I hadn't stolen anything. I even told her about my grandmother's death."

Robin leaned forward, just slightly.

"Lil looked right into my eyes for a few moments, then said she needed a chef for Charming Inn and was I interested." He held out his hands. "I said yes. I started working at the inn days later."

"So she believed you?"

"She did. She said she had an instinct that told her when to trust people, and she trusted me. I'll never forget that. Or forget what she did for me. It turned my whole life around."

"I see." Robin leaned back.

"So, do you believe me?" He searched her face, looking for some hint that she believed him, too.

Robin stared at him for a few moments before she answered. "It's not what you did or didn't do. It's that you never told me. It's a big thing in your life and explains a lot. But you never told me."

"What was I supposed to say? Hey Robs, by the way, I'm fresh out of jail?"

"You could have just told me the truth. Not

hidden it from me. I thought I knew you so well…"

"You do know me. Better than anyone." He started to reach for her hand but pulled back when he saw the shuttered look on her face.

"Except… I don't."

"I wish we could just go back to how things were. Friends." How had everything gotten so complicated for them?

"I need some time to process this."

"So you think I took the cash?"

"Back then, or Lillian's?"

"Either." He stared at her, willing her to say she believed him.

"Before all this happened, I would have said of course you didn't take it. Because I thought I knew you so well. But I don't. You've hidden so much about your past. So… how can I be sure about anything about you now?"

Her words cut him, stabbed his heart like a physical pain.

He stood. "Okay, then… I guess that is that." He also guessed there wasn't anything between them anymore. Not if she didn't believe him.

And why should she? She was right. He

hadn't trusted her enough to tell her about his past.

He walked away into the night.

ROBIN WALKED INTO THE BUNGALOW. She'd seen the hurt in Jay's eyes, but she couldn't just blindly say she believed him. Not after he'd hidden so much from her. She hadn't even known that his grandmother had raised him. He'd never told her that. He hadn't told her much of anything about his past. So how could they be good friends—or more—if he wouldn't even talk to her about his life? Where was the trust? And what else hadn't he told her?

She sank onto the couch and rested her chin in her hands. How had everything gotten so messed up?

She looked up when Charlotte came in. "Hey, you. Didn't think you'd still be up." Charlotte dropped her purse by the door and came over to sit on the couch.

"I'm up." She said without much enthusiasm.

"I ran into Camille at dinner tonight. She said the strangest thing about Jay being in jail for stealing and Sheriff Dave questioning him for the missing money from the inn." Charlotte kicked off her shoes. "So that's just Camille being Camille right?"

"No, Camille is telling the truth this time. And, of course, she can't wait to spread it all around town."

"Jay's been in jail?" Charlotte's forehead creased.

"Apparently."

"Did you know about it?"

"Nope." She shrugged. "And I thought I knew him so well. That we were getting close. I just found out he was raised by his grandmother, too. He never mentioned that with all the times he's said something was his grandmother's recipe."

"I guess he just wanted to keep the past in the past."

"Even with me? I thought we were getting close. We kissed. We had that wonderful day at Lighthouse Point and I thought we were headed toward some new level in our relationship. But I feel so foolish."

"Why?"

"Because I don't really know him and I was sure I did."

Charlotte leaned forward. "Sometimes it's hard to talk about our past. Remember how long it was before I told you about Reginald? That I'd been engaged to him and he stole from me? And you and Sara were my best friends, and I didn't tell you for the longest time."

"That was different."

"No, it was something I was embarrassed about and didn't want you to know." Charlotte cocked an eyebrow. "But you still felt like you knew me, right? I hadn't changed. It was just a piece of my past that I didn't share until I was ready."

Robin leaned back against the back of the couch. "But... I would have thought he would tell me important things. Like being raised by his grandmother and going to jail." She frowned. "He did look absolutely gutted when he told me about his grandmother dying while he was in jail."

"It probably hurts to talk about it."

"He also said he didn't steal from his last job. That he was innocent."

"Do you believe him?"

"He asked me that, but I told him I didn't know."

"Ouch, that had to hurt." Charlotte shook

her head. "He had a right to choose when to tell you. It was a hard story to tell."

"Lillian believes him." Robin sighed, confused, wanting things to just be... like they were before.

"And she's a good judge of character." Charlotte stood. "But you need to know in your heart you believe him, believe *in* him, and trust him. And then convince him you do. Otherwise, there's really not anything left between you two."

Charlotte went to her bedroom, and Robin sat on the couch. Is that what she wanted? Nothing left between her and Jay but co-workers? She'd always known he kept a hard shell around him. But underneath all that he was kind and gentle.

Trust.

Trust was... complicated.

JAY DIDN'T FEEL like going home to his empty house, so headed over to The Lucky Duck. He was glad to see Ben sitting at the bar. He slid onto a barstool beside his friend and ordered a beer.

Ben nodded at him. "I heard you had a bad day."

"You can say that again."

"I heard you had a bad day." Ben tossed him a wry grin.

"Very funny."

"So how is Sheriff Dave these days?"

"He's a jerk." He reached for the beer Willie handed him and nodded his thanks.

"Yep. Pretty much," Ben agreed. "So, rumor says Lillian found the missing money. The sheriff must have been disappointed. Crime spree averted. Now, what will he do?"

Jay looked at Ben. He didn't want to break Lillian's confidence and admit that Lillian had lied about finding the money. But then, he wasn't big on keeping secrets right now, either. Look what that had gotten him. He settled on "Lots of rumors in this town."

"Yes, sorry about that. Camille is having a great time spreading rumors about you."

"Yeah, well, they are probably the truth." He took a swig of his beer. "So, do you want to cut me out of your life, too? I never told you about the jail thing."

"Hey, your past is your past. All I know is

that you've been a great friend to me since you came to the island."

Jay raised his beer bottle, and Ben clinked his against it. "You're a good friend, Ben Hallet."

"How did Robin take the news?"

"Not well. She's mad that I never told her. There is so much I haven't told her about my past. I just… well, I liked keeping it in the past."

"It's a good place for it." Ben nodded.

"But now she says she didn't know me at all. Doesn't know me. Doesn't trust me."

"The timing could be better."

"You can say that again."

"The timing—" Ben grinned. "Sorry."

"I guess it doesn't matter. Robin deserves someone better than me. Who was raised in a normal family and hasn't been in jail. What do I know about relationships, anyway?"

"You're selling yourself short."

"No, just being honest. I don't know why I thought I could…" He shrugged. "That there could be something between Robin and I. Anyway, she doesn't believe me."

"Doesn't believe what?"

"That I never stole the money before. That I was innocent of what I went to jail for." He looked closely at Ben. "Though, I know that's what everyone says. That they're innocent."

"Hey, if you say you are, that's good enough for me."

"I appreciate that." They clinked bottles again, and he finally let the stress of the day begin to melt away.

At least he had Ben on his side. And Lillian. He always had Lillian on his side.

Just not Robin.

The one person he wanted to believe him.

CHAPTER 22

Lillian popped into Robin's office the next morning. Robin looked up and shook her head. "You're supposed to be taking the day off, remember?"

"I am... kind of."

"Right, sure looks like it. What's that in your hands?"

Lillian sheepishly looked down at the files in her hands. "Some orders I need to put in the computer?"

Robin reached out her hand. "Give them to me. I'll take care of it."

Lillian handed her the files. "Did Jay talk to you? I told him he should. Asked him to."

"So that's why he finally talked to me."

"I think he just hadn't found the right time before… before all of this mess."

"He did talk to me about his past. About how you found him at the restaurant and believed him."

"He didn't steal then and didn't now. It's that simple."

"The sheriff sounded like he thought Jay did it. I'm sure he'll keep questioning him."

Lillian shook her head. "No, he won't. I told him I found the money."

"You found it?"

"Well, no. But I wanted this all to disappear." Lillian shrugged. "Jay didn't take it and Sheriff Dave wasn't doing anything to find the real person who did. So I ended it."

"You lied to the sheriff to help Jay?"

"I just couldn't see that Sheriff Dave questioning Jay was going to do anything except make Jay feel bad, or get mad… or even decide to up and leave here. I couldn't blame him. Especially now that Camille is going around gossiping about him and his past."

"Camille is spreading rumors about Jay?" A surge of protectiveness swept through her. How dare Camille. That woman was nothing but trouble.

"She is. I guess my threats didn't do much to stop her. Not that I thought they would." Lillian sighed. "But I'm glad you know the truth now. Jay needs people to believe in him. He's a good man." She paused and narrowed her eyes. "You do believe him, right?"

"I— I'm just confused. I thought I knew him so well."

"Don't you know him? The kind of person he really is? None of this changes who he really is inside."

She slowly rose from behind the desk. "I know that you're right. I do. And I can't imagine Jay stealing anything from anyone. I was just so shocked to find out there was so much I didn't know about him."

Lillian shook her head. "You two are going to have to find a way to work this out. Or not. But I'll tell you one thing."

"What's that?"

"The man is hopelessly in love with you and has been for a long time. Whether you or he want to admit it."

She sat back down in her seat, her mouth open. "But—"

"I've known it for years. But I think Jay thought, because of his past, that he wasn't good enough for you. Which is nonsense. He's a good man. An honest man. A caring man under all that gruff facade."

Jay didn't *love* her. They'd only had that one day at Lighthouse Point. How could he love her? Lillian was wrong. She had to be.

"I hope you two work things out." Lillian turned to leave. "And, now, I'm headed to The Yarn Society. I wasn't going to go, but I think a little break in my schedule is just what I need right now."

Lillian disappeared and Robin stood staring at the empty doorway. Lillian had to be wrong. Jay didn't love her. And he certainly hadn't loved her for a long time. And right now, he didn't even *like* her.

LILLIAN WALKED into the community center and found her friends already chatting and knitting. Dorothy jumped up when she entered the room. "Lillian, we didn't think you were coming today. We figured you'd be busy with wedding to-dos."

Lillian hugged her friend. "I should be. But I just needed some non-inn, non-wedding time."

"You've come to the right place." Ruby patted the chair beside her. "Come sit down."

Lillian sat and took out her knitting. Soon the smooth motion did its magic and began to soothe her. Between the missing money, the sheriff questioning Jay, and all the wedding plans, she was about at her limit of stress she could handle.

"So, did you hear they've upped their prediction for this coming storm?" Dorothy paused her knitting. "Might hit as a hurricane instead of a tropical storm."

Apparently she hadn't yet hit her limit of stress. She frowned. "Are you sure? I thought I'd read it was getting weaker."

"It hung over the islands in the Caribbean and gained momentum overnight," Ruby added.

This was the last thing she needed. There was so much to be done to the inn if the storm was going to hit near here. Even if it hit further north, as predicted, the winds could do damage here and power could go out. What was she doing sitting here knitting with so much to do? She set her knitting in her lap.

"No, don't," Ruby said.

"Don't what?" Lillian looked at her friend.

"You were getting ready to pack up your knitting and leave. Stay for a bit and chat with us. Take some time and try to relax."

She let out a long sigh. "But there is so much to do."

"There's time. And, on the bright side, the weather is supposed to be lovely on Saturday. Not too hot and a light breeze. Perfect day for a wedding." Ruby nodded at her knitting. "Now, start knitting."

Lillian picked up her knitting again and soon the familiar rhythm of her needles did soothe her jangled nerves. "So what do you want to chat about?"

"Camille is going around spreading rumors." Dorothy shook her head. "That woman never quits, does she?"

"She asked if her invitation to the wedding got lost in the mail..." Lillian shook her head.

Dorothy laughed. "And what did you say to that?"

"That we were having a small wedding, just family and close friends."

"Of which you have *many*." Ruby smiled, her needles clicking away.

She did have many friends. Good ones. Like The Yarnies. She was a lucky woman. And soon, the day after tomorrow, she'd be married to Gary. Now if the storm would just dissipate everything would be perfect.

CHAPTER 23

The morning of Lillian's wedding dawned with a delicate pink light painted across the sky and streaks of lacy clouds. A perfect sunrise for a perfect day. Robin hurried along the sidewalk, headed to the inn. So much to do today. Charlotte had promised to come in soon and help with the setup. That was Charlotte's forte. Her own forte? Lists and checking off to-dos as near as she could figure.

She still hadn't seen much of Jay. He'd been busy preparing for the wedding. They'd only spoken about inn matters or wedding things and she could feel the mountain of unspoken words between them. Or maybe they'd already said all that needed to be said. But she couldn't think about that now. She just needed to concentrate on the wedding. Well, the wedding and also preparations for the coming storm. They'd had more cancellations for next week, and at this rate they'd have an almost empty inn. Bad for business, but it did make it easier to prepare for the storm.

She entered the inn and ran into Sara. "Sara, you're here early."

"Couldn't sleep. The list of things to do kept playing over and over in my head."

"Me, too." Robin laughed. "But first, I really need some coffee. Join me?"

"Oh, yes. Sounds great."

They headed to the kitchen to grab a couple cups of coffee. Robin glanced around, looking for Jay, and saw him over by the far counter, already at work. He looked up when they came in and gave her a small smile, then turned back to work. She shuttered her hurt feelings. But it was her fault anyway. She was the one who hadn't given him the words he needed to hear.

But she missed how they were before. She would have gone over to talk to him for a bit. He'd tease her about something. She missed the ease of it all, the conversations, and she missed walking home with him at night. She wasn't sure if they'd ever get back to that stage. A pang of loneliness twitched through her at the loss.

"You coming? I want to go find Aunt Lil." Sara stood waiting, her hands curled around her coffee cup.

"What? Yes, I'm coming." She poured herself a cup and headed out with Sara.

They found Lillian at The Nest, puttering in the kitchen. Sara walked over and kissed her aunt. "Morning. How are things here?"

"Just fine. I've been up for hours, though. I've straightened The Nest. Then straightened again. Gary will be staying here tonight before we head out on our honeymoon." Lil frowned. "I hate leaving with the storm coming."

"I'll take care of everything. Don't worry," Robin assured her.

But Lillian still looked worried.

"Let's just concentrate on your wedding day." Sara hugged Lil.

Robin pulled a long list out of her pocket. "See, I have my mobile list. Let's sit at the table and go through it. I want everything to be perfect." She looked over at Lil. "And absolutely no inn work for you today. None."

Lillian smiled as she sat down, but Robin was sure that if something came up, Lillian would jump in and take care of it. It was just the way she was.

Mason was glad his dad had decided against wearing a suit to the wedding. They were both wearing dress slacks and sports coats, but he planned on shucking the sports coat as soon as the wedding ceremony was over.

He'd prepared a best man speech, which had been amazingly hard for him. Here he could speak to a room filled with the board of directors, and he was the youngest man in the room. That didn't faze him a bit. But talking about his dad and Lillian? Well, that was hard. He still couldn't come up with an opening line to catch everyone's attention. He'd needed some witty stories to tell about his father... and he knew... none. The whole ordeal had been an exercise in frustration.

Now he'd left the speech... without an opening line... and walked around the inn, seeing if he could help with anything. He ran into Charlotte out on the deck, decorating for the reception.

"Need any help?"

"I've got this. But maybe they need your help setting up the chairs?"

He headed down to the beach and was pleased to find Zoe carting chairs from a stack and setting them up in rows.

"Need some help?" he asked as he walked up to her.

She gave him a big smile. "I sure could use help. Uncle Noah was helping me, but Sara pulled him away to do something. I promised I'd finish setting these up. Then Charlotte, who I guess is the talented bow-tier, is going to come put bows on each chair. Then we'll have mason jars of flowers lining the aisles."

He didn't understand the whole bows on chairs and all the little wedding details, but he did know how to set up chairs. Bonus that it was with Zoe.

They set up chair after chair, laughing and talking as they worked on their chore. Zoe was so easy to talk to. Her laugh charmed him. Her sparkling eyes captivated him. And he was ridiculously happy to have her for his date to the wedding.

They finished the last chair and sank onto two of them in the front row.

"I thought this was going to be a small wedding," he said.

"That's what everyone tries for here on the island. But everyone knows everyone, and the weddings seem to grow larger than expected."

"I get that. It does seem like everybody knows everybody here."

Zoe grinned. "They do. And they know everything about everybody, too. Not many secrets here on the island."

Mason stood as Charlotte walked up to them with a box full of bows. "I hope you're not wanting me to help with those."

Charlotte laughed. "No, I've got these."

"Then I better go find my dad and get him started on getting ready." He turned to Zoe. "I'll see you after the ceremony?"

"Sure will."

He walked away with the vision of Zoe's smile and her twinkling eyes firmly etched in his mind. He was looking forward to this wedding. Way more than he'd expected. Now if only he could think of that perfect opening line for his speech.

He found his father in his room, staring at his clothes. "Do you think I made the right decision? Maybe we *should* wear suits."

"Dad, we've been through this. You look snappy in your sports coat. Lillian said anything was fine with her."

"I still think I should go with my gray suit."

Mason rolled his eyes, then grinned. "Okay. Suits it is. Good thing I got them pressed, just in case. I'll go change and be back in a few minutes."

His dad nodded, looking distracted.

"You okay, Dad?"

"I'm fine. I'm just... well, I'm nervous." His dad gave him a sheepish grin. "You'd think at my age that I wouldn't be this nervous. I'm positive about my decision to marry Lil, it isn't that. I'm just... there will be so many changes for us. Living together. Sharing a space. Trying to figure out our work situations. And I still need to make up my mind about returning to the CEO position at GJ Industries."

Mason crossed back to his dad. "I don't think now is the time to worry about the CEO job. And I'm sure you and Lillian will work out sharing The Nest. It's all going to be fine."

"I've been on my own for a lot of years."

"And now you won't be. You'll have a wonderful woman by your side." Here he was giving a pep talk to his dad. Never thought that would happen.

His dad gave him a grateful smile. "You're right. Now you go get dressed, and I'll put on my suit and we'll do this wedding thing."

Mason walked out the door and down the hall to his own room. Weddings were... interesting. They brought out a bit of strangeness in people.

CHAPTER 24

Robin went to The Nest to meet up with Lillian, Sara, and Charlotte. The others were already there when she arrived. Lillian had put on her wedding dress and was standing in front of the mirror.

"Oh, Lillian, you're beautiful." Robin rushed over and gave her a quick hug, careful not to muss the dress.

"The dress turned out great, didn't it? Ruby did a fabulous job." Charlotte looked over every inch of Lillian's dress. "A very fabulous job. It's just perfect."

"I'm sure she'll do just as good of a job on your wedding dress," Sara said as she picked up a necklace and hooked it around Lillian's neck. "There. Perfect."

Charlotte looked over at Robin. "I told you that dress would look great on you, too. We did a good job picking it out."

"You did a good job picking it out. I just bought the one you told me to." She grinned at Charlotte.

"I'm so glad to have all you girls here. I'm glad you're all back on Belle Island." Lillian smiled.

"I'm glad to have them back, too," Robin agreed.

Lillian turned to face them. "You know, I waited until later in life to find my perfect match. Gary is just... well, he's perfect for me. And I'm so happy that Sara found Noah and Charlotte found Ben." Lillian turned to Robin. "And you and Jay found each other, too. You just need to work through this... bump. You're lucky to have found someone without waiting a lifetime like I did."

"Lil's right, you know. You and Jay... you're perfect for each other. Have you talked to him?" Sara asked.

"We've both been busy with the wedding."

"Don't let too much time go by, dear, or it will get harder and harder to try and work things out." Lillian gazed steadily at her.

"Promise me that you'll talk to him. Call it a little wedding present to me."

How could she refuse a request like that? She nodded. "I'll talk to him." If only she knew what she was going to say to him. "Now, let's finish getting Lillian ready." And talk about something else besides her and Jay.

LILLIAN STOOD at the end of the aisle, ready to step forward so Gary would see her, nervous, which was silly. What was there to be nervous about? She was too old for that nonsense, right? A mature woman didn't get nervous about things. Look at all she'd handled in her life. Why was she nervous now?

The aisle was beautifully lined with flowers in mason jars and teal bows on the chairs. Charlotte had done a wonderful job.

She took one more step and stood directly at the end of the aisle.

Gary looked up and saw her. A look of wonder—and did she see a hint of tears—filled his eyes. He held her gaze with his own. Suddenly she was no longer nervous.

"I'm ready," she said to Sara.

"I wish Mom were here to see this. She'd be so happy for you. *I'm* so happy for you." Sara squeezed her hand.

"I'm sure she is here with me. She wouldn't miss it." Lillian looked up at the sky and saw a blue heron slowly glide by with steady strokes of its wings. She smiled. Yes, Leah was here with her.

She took Sara's arm and they walked down to the arbor, aunt and niece, two women who'd been extremely lucky to find love this year. Her heart swelled with happiness. For herself. For Sara. Well, probably for *everyone* today.

Gary extended his hand when she reached him, and she clasped his hand in hers. Connecting them. Ready for what the future would bring.

The actual ceremony passed in a blur. All she knew was Gary was right by her side, her hand in his.

"You may now kiss the bride."

"You bet." Gary grinned and leaned down to give her a good, long kiss. Then another. The guests laughed and clapped.

Joy bubbled through her and her heart sang with happiness. A blissful contentment settled around her.

She walked back down the aisle again, this time with Gary at her side, as he would be for the rest of their lives. Her husband. When they got to the end of the aisle, Gary leaned close to her.

"I will never forget this day, or how I feel right now at this very moment."

She would never forget it either. She didn't need the wedding photos to remind her. It was engraved in her memory forever. The perfect day. Marrying the perfect man for her.

"I love you," she whispered back, and he smiled.

CHAPTER 25

Z oe wandered around the reception, catching up with old friends from town, but keeping an eye out for Mason. He finally came up to her—without his suit coat on—after he'd given his toast. "Hey, you."

"Hi. You did a great job with your speech."

"You think? I was nervous about it."

"Great opening line and you didn't look nervous."

"Good. I faked it well, then." He gave her one of his now-familiar impish grins. "Do you want to dance?"

"I do."

He held out his hand and she took it and followed him to the dance floor where a spirited oldie rock song was playing. It finished right as they got to the floor and a slow love song came on.

He wrapped an arm around her waist and took her hand in his as he pulled her close and started to sway to the music. She danced near to him, slowly, feeling the heat of him, and she swore she could hear his heart beating even though there was still space between them.

Until there wasn't.

He pulled her closer and she rested her head against this shoulder, lost in the music, lost in the moment. Ignoring the thumping of her own heart. Her racing pulse. The flutter in her stomach. Yes, ignoring all of that.

This was ridiculous. She'd just met him. And really, he lived about as far away as he could from her in the U.S. unless he decided to move to Alaska.

But her traitorous heart continued to pound, and she cursed her luck. She was fully aware she was falling for this man. And that was a ridiculous thing to do. A dangerous thing to do. Dangerous to her heart. He was leaving in a few days. He'd be in Washington, and she'd be in Florida.

But, even though it was silly, she pushed the reasons aside and decided to just enjoy the moment. And, boy, was she enjoying the moment.

JAY LOOKED AROUND THE KITCHEN, making sure everything was put away. It was late, and he'd have to be back early in the morning. But the wedding had been great. The food had been good if he did say so himself. He'd outdone himself trying to make Lillian proud, and she'd complimented the food multiple times.

He'd seen Robin a few times, chatting with guests, making sure everyone was taken care of. And she'd sat with Sara and Charlotte for a good long time later in the evening. Those women. Quite a threesome. He couldn't imagine having lifelong friends like that. He was even a bit jealous of what they had. But his life hadn't been conducive to making friends. First, his mother had dragged him around from state to state, then dumped him on his grandmother's doorstep like some kind of extraneous baggage. But those years with his grandmother had been some of the best of his life.

The familiar sadness seeped through him at the thought of her. The if-onlys. If only she were still alive. If only she could see him now, see that he'd made a name for himself, at least on the island.

Though, he *had* seen people staring at him tonight. The rumor mill had already been running strong, that much was obvious. The old Jay would have just pulled up stakes and moved on. But he wasn't going to leave Lillian. So he ignored the stares and went about his own business. Things were different now, but he owed Lillian so much. He'd stay and be her chef and do his best to ignore the talk and the stares.

He'd hoped that Robin would drop in and make sure everything had gone well tonight, or maybe even compliment the food. But, no. No Robin.

He hung up his apron and walked out, locking the door behind him, adjusting to his new normal of walking home alone.

CHAPTER 26

Lillian woke up the next morning with Gary by her side. It was unfamiliar, and yet comforting. The sun streamed in the windows as if contradicting the weatherman's forecast of the coming storm.

"Morning." Gary's rumbly voice welcomed her.

She smiled at him. "Morning."

"How does it feel being a married woman?"

"It feels nice." She sat up in bed and stretched.

Gary reached over to his night table and picked up an envelope. "Here, this is for you." He sat up next to her.

"What is it?"

"Open it."

She opened it and read the card and the note he'd written. "We're going to an island in the Caribbean?"

"We are. A small island. We'll have part of it all to ourselves. I have a private jet waiting for us. We'll be gone for two glorious weeks. Just you and me. Well, there's a chef there and some help, but they'll come in and then disappear. I can't wait."

She glanced over at her open suitcase in the corner. He'd said to pack for warm weather, and she had. She just hadn't known it would be this... special. This... exceptional. He'd gone to so much trouble to figure out every little detail.

"We can leave whenever you're ready. I thought maybe we'd go to the dining room and get some breakfast, then head out."

"That sounds nice." And it did. But she was worried about leaving the inn for two weeks. Especially with the storm coming. But he'd gone to so much trouble to set this all up, so she smiled at him. "Very nice."

They got ready and headed to the dining room. She paused when they got to the lobby. "I need to stop by my office for just one thing. Can I meet you in the dining room?"

"Sure thing. Don't be long. And don't let

Robin see you. You're not supposed to be working." He kissed her and headed to the dining room.

She slipped into her office and turned on the computer. A quick search of the weather showed they were now definitely predicting the storm to become a hurricane. It was still supposed to hit north, but now the uncertainty of the exact area it would hit had grown. It could actually hit Belle Island directly. Worry coursed through her. She couldn't leave the inn with the storm coming. But she couldn't disappoint Gary and just cancel their honeymoon.

She looked up to see Robin and Gary standing in the doorway.

"You're not supposed to be working." Robin scowled.

"I was just… checking the weather," she said guiltily.

Robin sighed. "I saw the change. But you never know. Hurricanes are unpredictable. You two should get out of here while the weather is still nice enough to fly."

Gary stepped into the room. "Lillian?"

She looked at him, unable to say the words.

He came around to her side of the desk,

took her hands, and helped her stand. "So, I guess we're going to postpone the honeymoon, huh?"

"What?" She looked directly at him.

"Lil, it's obvious you're worried about the inn. I don't blame you. I understand you not wanting to leave with the storm coming."

"But, you made all these special plans."

He kissed her on the cheek. "And I'll make them again. Later. After the storm."

She clasped both his hands in hers. "Are you sure?"

"I'm sure. Looks like we have a lot of work ahead getting ready for the storm. You just put me to work."

Her heart filled with gratitude for this man who knew her so well and was willing to give up so much. She reached up and touched his cheek. "Thank you. I do love you."

He winked at her. "That's a good thing because I heard a rumor that you just married me."

CHAPTER 27

Zoe sat across from Mason at breakfast in the dining room. She'd had such a good time last night and had been pleased when he'd asked her to have breakfast with him and spend the day at the beach. She could still almost feel his arms around her like when they were dancing. It had been a magical night. And lasted until two in the morning when he'd finally walked her up to her room.

As long as she had this crush on him, she might as well enjoy the day. It was only a little crush, though. He fascinated her. She loved his impossibly impish grin and the one dimple it highlighted. She loved talking to him. Laughing with him. And time just seemed to sweep by when she was with him.

Too bad today would be their last day together. He was heading out to Seattle tomorrow and she was heading back to Orlando.

Mason ordered waffles, bacon, and a side of hash browns. She ordered one of Jay's cinnamon rolls and coffee. Lots of coffee. She wasn't used to only a few hours of sleep, but it didn't seem to bother Mason. He was chipper and alert this morning.

Mason wolfed his breakfast down like he hadn't had plate after plate of food at the reception. And he had. She'd seen him. How did men eat like that and stay in such incredible shape? Mason was in good shape. He must work out at the gym or something.

She should think about joining a gym. She no longer had the beach for her long beach walks, and she didn't really get much exercise now. There, that was decided. She'd join a gym.

"What you thinking about?" Mason asked.

She looked at him trying to figure out what words to say so she didn't sound like an unfit sloth. "Oh, nothing. Just thinking about things that need to be done when I get back home."

"Yes, my flight leaves early tomorrow. Have

to get back and put out the brushfires that came up while I was here."

Lillian and Gary walked up to them, hand in hand. "Morning, son. Zoe."

"Morning." They both said in unison and she smiled.

"You two off soon?" Mason asked.

"About that." Gary paused, smiled at Lillian, then turned back to Mason. "I appreciate all your help with the surprise, but it appears that we're not going to go on a honeymoon right now."

"You're not?" Mason frowned.

"With the storm coming, it seems like a better idea to stay here. It looks like there's a possibility it might hit nearer to Belle Island now. And Lillian would just worry about the inn if we left. I promised her we'd reschedule it for later."

Lillian's eyes softened as she looked at Gary. "And your father is a very understanding man."

Zoe watched the looks between Lillian and Gary. So much love. So much understanding and compromise. She wanted that with someone. Sometime, she wanted that.

"Anyway, since the jet is fueled and ready, I thought you could just take it back to Seattle today. Get out before the storm. No need to wait for your commercial flight tomorrow. The jet needs to be back in Seattle this next week anyway."

"I... uh..." Mason looked at her.

Did she see disappointment in the depths of those eyes of his? She gave him a weak smile.

"That makes sense to go back today."

"Okay, then. I'll give the pilot a call and head back home today."

"Good." Gary nodded. "Now, I'm headed off with Lillian to help with preparing for the storm. Something about a million hurricane shutters to put up."

Lillian and Gary walked away, and Zoe looked at Mason. "That's good that you'll get out before the storm."

"I guess. I'm sorry about today though. I was looking forward to spending it with you."

"Me, too." Really looking forward to it. But then, this moment had to come eventually, didn't it? Their lives were on opposite sides of the country.

They finished their meal and headed to the lobby as she counted her seconds with him.

Which. Was. Silly.

"I'm going to head up and pack. You going to be around in about twenty minutes?"

"Yes."

"Let me pack and I'll meet you back here in the lobby. I'd like to say goodbye before I head out."

She nodded and watched him hurry up the stairs to his room. She went to stand by the window. Hard to believe a storm was coming with the brilliant blue sky and fluffy white clouds out there today. But she'd seen it before. That was life in Florida. Always keeping an eye on a developing storm. There would be so much work to do to get the inn ready. And she really should offer to help Noah get the community center all ready, too. She'd go over there after Mason left.

After Mason left.

The thought filled her with sadness. She shook her head slightly. It was what it was.

Mason was back in fifteen minutes, pulling his suitcase behind him. "There you are. Walk me out?"

She nodded and walked outside with him and over to his rental car. He swung the suitcase in the trunk and turned to her. "Zoe, I had a really good time this week. Unexpected, but really nice."

She gave him a small smile. "I did, too."

"I… well, there's something I've been wanting to ask you. Something I've been wanting to do."

"What's that?"

"I was hoping to… kiss you."

Her eyes widened. "You were?"

"Yes…" His eyes darkened with a hopeful glint.

Her breath quickened and she nodded the slightest movement of her head. He reached out a hand and cupped her cheek, then leaned in closer. He kissed her. Tentatively at first, but then he kissed her until she was breathless.

She grabbed hold of both of his arms, steadying herself, savoring every moment of the kiss.

He pulled away. "That was…" He tossed her that impish grin. "That was a very nice kiss."

"It was." She smiled back at him.

"Fate is funny sometimes, isn't it? I came for my dad's wedding, and instead, I found you. I had a really great week."

"Me, too."

He reached out and brushed her cheek with his knuckles. "I'll miss you, Zoe. Take care." His mouth curved into a reluctant smile. "And I'm only six hours away by jet."

He slipped into his car and pulled away. She stood in the shade under a palm tree, staring after where the car had disappeared, feeling an emptiness settle over her. Stifling her. Smothering her.

Fate was funny sometimes. She was sorry to see him go. He fascinated her. She let out a long sigh.

Of course, she'd finally fall for a guy... and he was a six-hour plane trip away. It figured.

CHAPTER 28

R obin had promised Lillian that she'd talk to Jay. And she would. When it was the right time. Now, with all the storm prep, it didn't seem like the right time. Or maybe she just wasn't ready yet.

She took a break mid-afternoon to go back to the bungalow and check on their hurricane shutters there. She hated putting them up. They had the kind that screwed on with wing nuts and it drove her crazy screwing them all on. Then repeating the process to take them down. Ugh, how she hated it.

Most of the shutters were metal, but they had a few almost clear ones so a bit of light would come into the bungalow. She hated the dark, dim days, waiting for storms. But she'd waited for many storms during her life here on the island. This was just one more. With the stupid hurricane shutters.

She stood in the garage looking at the despised shutters. She'd put a handful of them up now. Then maybe she and Charlotte could finish up later.

"I'll help."

She whirled around at the sound of Jay's voice.

"I know how you hate putting them up. Lillian said you'd headed back here to get started. I figured I'd give you a hand."

"You don't have to do that."

"I want to."

She stared at him for a moment. "Okay, then. I do hate putting them up." They each grabbed a shutter and headed out to the side of the bungalow. Mrs. Gleason sat on her porch with a suitcase by her side. Barney lounged beside her.

"I should go say something to Mrs. Gleason."

"I'll come with you."

They crossed over to Mrs. Gleason's porch. "Are you leaving?" Robin pointed toward the suitcase.

"Yes, my daughter is coming to pick me up. Wants me off the island because of the storm. And then she's moving me into the retirement center. And we're dropping Barney off with the lady who runs the beagle rescue. They promised they'd find him a good home. But he'll be with strangers." Tears filled the woman's eyes.

"I'll take Barney." Jay stepped forward.

"You'll take him?" Robin and Mrs. Gleason asked in unison.

"Sure, Barney and I get along great. I'd like to have a buddy at my house. I mean, if you want me to take him. And you could come visit him whenever you wanted. Or I could even bring him over to see you when I have time off."

Mrs. Gleason stood up. "Are you sure? You want to take him?"

"I'm sure. We'll be great buds, won't we Barney?" The dog wagged his tail.

"Oh, that's so wonderful." Mrs. Gleason threw her arms around Jay's neck and hugged him.

Jay blushed. Blushed. Robin smiled. Jay Turner was a good man.

She stared at him for a long moment. He *was* a good man. A very good one. And she was a fool.

CHAPTER 29

Jay gathered the box of dog supplies from Mrs. Gleason's porch and brought it over to Robin's, then returned to say goodbye to the woman as she got in her daughter's car. He pressed a piece of paper with his phone number into Mrs. Gleason's hand.

"Call any time to check up on Barney. And I promise we'll come visit after the storm, okay?"

Mrs. Gleason reached a hand out the window and touched his arm. "I'll be forever grateful."

"And I'll take good care of him," he assured her, then watched as they drove away.

Robin stood on Mrs. Gleason's porch watching him. "You're a good man, Jay."

"I just thought it was about time to get a dog. Tired of rattling around that empty house. Besides, Barney is great."

"Except when he's eating my shoes," she said dryly.

"He won't eat mine, will you, Barney?" The dog stood and stretched.

"Don't count on it. But it was a very nice thing to do for Mrs. Gleason. She's so worried about him. And now she'll get to see him, too."

He shrugged, uncomfortable with the compliments.

She stepped off the porch and walked up to him. "Jay... can we talk?"

"We did talk, remember?" He didn't think rehashing everything was where he wanted to go.

"Can we talk again?"

He let out a sigh. "Sure. I guess."

They returned to Robin's and sat on the chairs on the front porch. Barney settled at his feet and he petted the dog. He was going to have to make some adjustments in his life. Pop home more often to let the dog out. Luckily Dana was working out. He could probably start a schedule where they both weren't working together so much. He could take some time off.

Robin sat patiently waiting for him to look at her. He knew she'd wait until he looked at her before she started talking. It's what she did. He finally gave in and looked her way.

"Jay… I was upset when I found out all that about you. So much I didn't know."

"We've been through this before, Robs."

"Hear me out." She held up a hand. "I was… foolish. I reacted badly. I let the surprise of it get to me. I hate surprises."

"I know that about you."

"And you had every right to keep your past to yourself. To pick the time to tell me. And I do think you would have eventually told me."

"I would have. And I actually came to tell you. Right after the money went missing. So you could hear it from me. But… you were with Mason." He scratched Barney's head. "And I didn't tell you about my grandmother because… well, honestly, Robs, it hurts to talk about her. I still miss her every single day."

She reached out and touched his arm. "I'm sure you do. And I'm sorry for your loss."

He nodded, staring down at her hand on his arm with the pink nails and the thin silver bracelet encircling her wrist. There it was again. The details. Noticing every little detail. And he wasn't sure he wanted to notice them. Not anymore.

But then she jumped up and crossed the porch to lean on the railing. "I— I owe you such an apology. I've been so wrapped up in how I feel, how it all surprised me. I should have been thinking about how all this affected you. How *you* felt."

Now, these were words he hadn't planned on hearing.

"Jay, of course, you didn't take the money. Not Lillian's. Not the other money. You aren't that person." She paced down the porch and came back. "I know the real Jay. I trust the real Jay. I—I care about the real Jay."

He swallowed. Swallowed hard.

"Jay, can you please, please forgive me? Give me another chance?"

"You believe me?" He just wanted to make sure he'd heard correctly.

"Of course I do. I really do."

He looked at her. "And I should have trusted you more. Told you all about my past a long time ago. It was just such a hard discussion to have."

"So, we'll have no more secrets?" She looked

right into his eyes, not wavering for a second, and he felt his heart swell.

"No more secrets, Robs. You know everything now."

"So, we're going to try this again, right?" She grinned at him, her heart filling with... something. Was it love? She wasn't certain, but she *was* certain she wanted to find out. "You know that no one ever wins an argument with me. You might as well give in."

He grinned right back at her. "Well, since no one wins an argument with you, I won't argue." He jumped up, took her hands, and pulled her to her feet. He wrapped his arms around her and pulled her close. "I've been wanting to do that for days."

She leaned against him, drinking in the feeling of being in his arms again, listening to his heart beat against her cheek she pressed to his chest. "And I've been wanting that, too."

He tilted her head up and she looked into his eyes. "Robs, let's try not to mess it up this time."

"Fine by me."

"And now I'm going to get that kiss I've been wanting ever since we had that picnic at Lighthouse Point. And I want to go out on a date. A proper date. And everyone can see us, I don't care. I don't want you to date Mason or anyone else. It's been five years or so, Robs. Time enough. Now it's time for us."

She closed her eyes and he kissed her right there on the front porch, for all the world—or the town—to see. She forgot all about the coming storm and whatever had torn them apart. Because now they were back together. And with his kiss… with his kiss she was certain it *was* love she felt for this man.

"And one more thing…" Jay pulled back slightly. "I love you, Robs. So I wasn't going to argue with you anyway."

And he kissed her again.

DEAR READER, I hope you enjoyed this story. Now, are you ready to read more about Robin and Jay? And what about Anna, the journal writer? We need to know if Lillian ever finds out what happened to Anna, right? Okay, one more question… who stole the money?

Try Book Six - **Six Hours Away** to get the answers to all these questions!

in the multi-author Indigo Bay series. The three stories are all interconnected.

Sweet Days by the Bay

Or buy them separately:

Sweet Sunrise - Book Three

Sweet Holiday Memories - A short holiday story

Sweet Starlight - Book Nine

ABOUT THE AUTHOR

Kay writes sweet, heartwarming stories that are a cross between women's fiction and contemporary romance. She is known for her charming small towns, quirky townsfolk, and enduring strong friendships between the women in her books.

Kay lives in the Midwest of the U.S. and can often be found out and about with her camera, taking a myriad of photographs which she likes to incorporate into her book covers. When not lost in her writing or photography, she can be found spending time with her ever-supportive husband, knitting, or playing with her puppies —two cavaliers and one naughty but adorable Australian shepherd. Kay and her husband also love to travel. When it comes to vacation time, she is torn between a nice trip to the beach or the mountains—but the mountains only get considered in the summer—she swears she's allergic to snow.

Learn more about Kay and her books at kaycorrell.com

While you're there, sign up for her newsletter to hear about new releases, sales, and giveaways.

WHERE TO FIND ME:
kaycorrell.com
authorcontact@kaycorrell.com

Join my Facebook Reader Group. We have lots of fun and you'll hear about sales and new releases first!
https://www.facebook.com/groups/KayCorrell/

I love to hear from my readers. Feel free to contact me at authorcontact@kaycorrell.com

facebook.com/KayCorrellAuthor
instagram.com/kaycorrell
pinterest.com/kaycorrellauthor
amazon.com/author/kaycorrell
bookbub.com/authors/kay-correll